Ocotillo
Dreams

Melinda Palacio

Bilingual Press/Editorial Bilingüe
Tempe, Arizona

Library of Congress Cataloging-in-Publication Data

Palacio, Melinda.
  Ocotillo dreams / Melinda Palacio.
      p. cm.
  ISBN 978-1-931010-75-7 (hardcover : alk. paper) — ISBN 978-1-931010-76-4
(soft cover : alk. paper)
  1. Chandler (Ariz.)—Fiction. 2. Illegal aliens—Arizona—Fiction. 3.
Emigration and immigration—Political aspects—United States—Fiction. 4.
Mothers and daughters—Fiction. 5. Mexican Americans—Race identity—
Fiction. I. Title.
  PS3616.A3385O36 2011
  813'.6—dc22
                                                        2011005542

PRINTED IN THE UNITED STATES OF AMERICA

Front cover art: The Dreamer *(2002) by Patssi Valdez*

Cover and interior design by Bill Greaves

For Blanca Estela Palacio

Contents

Acknowledgments

The first person I must acknowledge is my mother, Blanca Estela Palacio (1949–1994), for encouraging me to embrace life with every ounce of joy and passion in my being. My grandmother, Maria Victoria Ibarra Gutierrez, instilled her love of storytelling. My grandfather Juan Gutierrez taught me how to laugh at life. I acknowledge everyone who gave me a boost along the way, especially my mother's sister Rosa Carmen and their eight brothers, Juan, Eloy, Henry, Manuel, Oscar, Mario, Tony, and Raymond Gutierrez, who taught me how to swim and survive a rough world. Mary Rose and Edward R. Ortega introduced me to books by Chicano authors.

Of my friends and family, the journey of writing poetry, short stories, news articles, and a debut novel would not be possible without Emily Palacio, the Baers, Fredda and Nydia Olivares, Ralph Serrano, Xochitl Avellán, Valarie Neiman, Katey O'Neill, Susan Chiavelli, Karen Telleen-Lawton, Karin Finell, Harriet Ackert, Mary Brown, Josie Martin, Jim Alexander, Lora Martin, Jocelyn M. Kremer, Karl Bradford, Flavia Valle, Alison Schaumburg, Sojourner K. Rolle, Linda Stewart-Oaten, Grace Rachow, Toni Lorien, Ned Bixby, Gail Knight, Laura Mattingly, Melanie Leavitt, Nancy Harris, John Travis, and the blogueros at La Bloga, including Daniel Olivas, Michael Sedano, and Manuel Ramos.

Seeds for *Ocotillo Dreams* were planted during my years as a freelance journalist for the East Valley and Scottsdale Tribune. I turned to journalism after S. Yao and I lived in Chandler, Arizona. When I returned to California, Martha Lannan hired me as a reporter for the Goleta Valley Voice. The assignment allowed me to meet Denise Chávez, who welcomed me to the Mesilla Cultural Center in New Mexico. Denise introduced me to so many wonderful people who have moved me to work on my craft, including Pat Minjárez, Luis Urrea, Martín Espada, Alex Espinoza, Malín Alegría, Cristina García, Quincy Troupe, and Daniel Zolinksy.

As a Santa Barbara Writers Conference (SBWC) volunteer, I had the pleasure of meeting Mary and Barnaby Conrad, and later Marcia Meier. At the SBWC, I won two writing awards and received valuable comments on my early fiction and poetry from Barnaby Conrad, Catherine Ryan-Hyde, Laura Taylor, Sid Stebel, Christopher Moore, Phyllis Gebauer, Matt Pallamary, Yvonne Nelson Perry, John M. Daniel, Monte Schulz, Perie Longo, David Starkey, Barry Spacks, and Karen Ford. The trinity of Lions, Anne and Shelly Lowenkopf and Leonard Tourney, were fierce in their belief in this story.

I benefited from an incredible year in 2007 when I received the PEN USA Emerging Voices Rosenthal Fellowship. Leslie Schwartz mentored me, Christine Lanoie set the schedule, Luis Rodríguez inspired me, and Adam Sommers directed the show. EV fellows Reyna Grande, Sandra Ramírez Thomas, and Avi Lall offered much appreciated criticism. An excerpt of *Ocotillo Dreams* appears in the PEN EV Anthology, 2010.

For the publishing of this book, I am grateful to everyone at Bilingual Press and the Hispanic Research Center at Arizona State University, especially Gary Francisco Keller, Karen Van Hooft, Amy Phillips, and my editor, Linda St. George. Finally, this book would not be possible without the love and support of my exceptional husband, Steve Beisner.

Prologue

Red. Her mother's favorite color. Long ago, in her mother's kitchen, red danced on dish towels, tablecloths, the ristra of dried red chiles rattled the hallway, the sound of red, tomato red of her mother's salsa, tongue-burning red. Red posture, red perfume, red footsteps. Red was the color on her mother's toenails when Isola arrived at the Maricopa County Hospital to claim the body. Red was the color of her plane ticket.

A strange trip to make with an estranged dead mother. She had accompanied the body back to San Francisco where she buried her mother with sprays of red roses. Isola became dizzy when the funeral director led her through the showroom's hospital smell and suffocating maze of coffins. The tall lady in the blazer said she'd make things easy and pointed to a white casket crowned with red roses. Our finest, the lady had said. Isola wondered what that meant. Red heels and a red dress with a flared skirt for the burial and viewing: her mother's bon voyage in second-hand clothes. Isola had used her own favorite outfit to bury her mother. Only the lipstick troubled her. Her mother wore cherry that never smudged. Isola undertook a frantic search for the right shade of red, a deep color that would last forever.

Red was the color of the ocotillo's flower. Her mother always sent the same postcard with an ocotillo in bloom. The cursive writing below the ocotillo haunted her. *Welcome to Chandler, AZ, Where Ocotillo Dreams Come True.* She studied the postcard, memorized each red bloom and thorn as if the cactus might transport her to her mother. Isola read the last postcard over and over again. She and her mother were tied to this earth by a thin thread. An invisible string from San Francisco to the desert, however fragile, was all they had needed. A new postcard would've been due next month. Her correspondences with her mother had started to take on a friendlier tone. The last postcard mentioned a possible visit to San Francisco. Isola remembered muttering to herself, *that will never happen.* Cassandra's prophecy came true on a postcard from Chandler, Arizona. The glimmer of hope for a normal relationship, one not left to guessing and disappointment, gone. Even more painful was her not having a clue about how ill her mother had been. Isola was left with nothing but unanswered questions and a stack of postcards of ocotillo dreams.

Cruz waited until dusk to continue his long trek across the desert. In the distance he saw a single ocotillo, its tips so red that the plant looked as though it were bleeding. A Snickers bar was his last bit of food until he reached El Norte. He closed his eyes and savored the sticky chocolate on his lips. When he looked up he wondered why he hadn't noticed the woman seated under the ocotillo or that the red of the ocotillo flower was real blood. The woman's hair and face were bloody. Her thin, curvy form and long hair reminded him of his brother's wife, Rosalina, the most beautiful woman in all of México. The woman rocked herself and sang the song his mother always sang. The last time she had sung the song, his mother cried and said she might never see him again. He felt love. The scent of his mother's kitchen, cinnamon and tortillas, drifted through the desert air. The song faded into a lullaby he'd never heard before. The sweet music drew him closer to the woman rocking herself under the ocotillo. She was not his mother, nor anyone he knew. But he was certain he loved her more than he'd ever loved anyone.

Cruz cried for the woman. His tongue was numb and bleeding from his own bite. He had lost her.

I

The
House

1

The House

Chandler, Arizona, 1997

She made her way downstairs. At 3:00 in the morning the white light from the fridge was offensive. A thumping noise came from the corner of the kitchen. She wasn't alone. "Huhah." She jumped. Her heart pumped louder and faster. She turned to see a man in jeans, sandals, and a blanket draped over his chest, curled up on the window seat. His hands and toes twitched as if dreaming. Think. Think. Breathe, she reminded herself. She feared passing out from sheer fear if she didn't breathe. Breathe, she told herself again. She froze, but wanted to scream. The man snored lightly. Her legs were numb, but she was able to move her head enough to scan the room for a weapon. Knock him out, call the police. She'd seen it in a movie. But Isola had no idea where her mother had kept her kitchen knives or other potential weapons. She grabbed her water bottle from the freezer and switched on the lights.

"Don't move. I called the police." She held her cold weapon above her head.

The man screamed and sat up.

She straightened her back, made herself taller, and threw the frozen bottle at him. He caught it. "The police are on their way." She made her voice sound strong and commanding. She turned to look for a knife. A pair of metal tongs was all she managed. "Don't move." She waved the flimsy kitchen utensil high above her head as though wielding a medieval sword.

The man cowered in the window seat. "No. Por el amor de Dios. No le llame a la policía."

5

"Stay right there. No move, no muevas." She struggled for the Spanish word. She continued to scream a gibberish of English and Spanish threats. "Para—don't—stop—hombre—muy bad—I swear."

"Por favor. No policía. Por favor," he pleaded above her screams. His hands hovered in front of his chest in a surrendering gesture. She was calm enough to hear him talking to her. He was saying her name. "Isola." He spoke slowly, elongating her name. "Iee—soo—laah," he said.

"Who are you? How do you know my name?" She rubbed the numbness out of her fingers. Her heart resumed a slower pace.

The man settled back onto the window seat. Loose threads around the edges of bright yellow curtains grazed his hair.

"You're doña Marina's daughter," he said in Spanish. "You teach at a university. You read books. You rent an apartment from doña Marina's German friend in San Francisco." He spoke quickly, as though bartering for his life.

She flinched at his recital of her life story.

"Who are you?"

"Cruz. Me llamo Cruz Zárate. Por favor, no llame a la policía."

She hunched her shoulders and waved away his concern, as she realized he was another one of her mom's projects. The patch of gray above Cruz's ears made him look older than Isola. But what's a few years? I'm glad Mom found the son she had always wanted, Isola thought.

"I won't call the police," she said. She sat down at the table to cover her bare legs. She felt naked in her long T-shirt and underwear.

He took a deep breath. Isola watched his fear abate. His softened face was like a rumpled shirt. He was handsome, she thought. A deeper glance and she noticed he had a striking resemblance to the Venezuelan singer El Puma; his thick hair was almost two inches longer than her own shorn bob. He blushed. She knew he had caught her staring at him. He looked down at his jeans. She looked away.

"You knew my mother?" she said in Spanish. The language of her mother started to roll more freely from her tongue.

He nodded. Of course he had known her mother. They both nodded and smiled. Stayed serene and comforted for a while. If he knew so much about her, he must know even more about her mother's life in the desert, a world unfamiliar to her.

"Lo siento, era muy buena, su madre." His smile faded.

He gave her a look of pity, the kind she had seen over and over again, the same look people had given her and her mother when they had buried her father. She was not allowed to turn away from the faces of sympathy or the obligatory hugs and kisses strangers gave her. She knew the drill and offered Cruz her hand. He clasped his warm hands over hers, gently enclosing her palm. She held her breath during the silent offering to her mother's memory.

"I'm a mess." She pulled away. "I'll make coffee."

Cruz watched Isola fill the carafe with water and search the cabinets for coffee. She opened every drawer, looked in the refrigerator and underneath the sink. He hesitated to help. The view of her legs in tight jeans bewitched him. He watched and studied her. Watched her lips moving. Watched her take down two ceramic cups and rinse them. He didn't want to admit that he knew where the coffee was, that he had helped himself to her mother's kitchen.

"I'm not sure there's any grounds." Isola riffled through more drawers.

She bit her lip and ran her fingers through her hair too many times. She looked as if she wanted to scream. Cruz had seen that breaking point on the face of Marina and his own mother. He knew if he didn't step up to help, she'd lose her good humor. Finally, he went to her side and opened two cabinets before taking a crumpled bag from the freezer.

Isola made a funny face. "Of course, Mom always kept coffee in the freezer." She snatched the coffee from his loose grip.

Cruz didn't catch everything she was saying, but he enjoyed looking at her. Except for Marina's long gray hair, which she had always kept in a tight bun, mother and daughter looked alike and moved in the same way. The wide Mexican nose softened by high cheekbones, a short figure in caramel skin. He remembered Marina mentioning that Isola's father had dark skin for an Anglo. Despite her accent, green eyes, and the way she made certain simple words sound foreign, as though she were speaking Chinese, Isola looked to be pure Mexican to him. Even though her hair was too short, she was beautiful.

The coffee bubbled in the machine. Cruz inhaled the earthy aroma of the dark coffee beans.

Isola sat at the round table and took a deep breath. "Why were you sleeping in the kitchen?"

"Perdón," he said. "I'm sorry to bother you." He had been so stupid for not checking the house this time. Cruz didn't know how to explain everything to her in one sentence. He put his thoughts together, but didn't know where to start.

"It's OK." Isola picked up the yellow cup by the handle and examined it as though it might turn into a bird and fly away. "Tell me why you were sleeping here and how you know my mother." She poured his coffee and added cream and sugar.

Cruz warmed his hands on the big round cup. Isola fixed coffee just like her mother, with lots of sugar. He eyed her as he tasted a stronger sip, as though drinking her scent along with the rich beans.

"I can pour that out if you want it black."

He smiled. "No, está rico." He took a big sip to show her how good the coffee was. "Your mother helped people like me who cross the border."

"She helped you cross the border? She was a coyote?"

Cruz laughed. "No era coyote. She helped with English classes and jobs and many things." He wanted to tell her about Marina's work with the Rescate Ángeles, but Marina had once asked him never to mention the group to her daughter. He had to respect her wishes.

"Why were you sleeping in the kitchen?"

"I thought the house was empty. It is an easy place to sleep before I go to la barda to find work." He didn't say anything about the dreams that awoke him when he slept in the kitchen, how the window seat seemed easier and less intrusive than the couch or bed upstairs.

"You mean you don't have a place to stay?"

"Yes, I have. I stay with my friend's aunt, but her house is very crowded. Doña Trinidad has a big family and many dogs. The house is always full of cousins, aunts, and friends."

"I can understand you coming here for some privacy," Isola said. "But why sleep in the kitchen?" She looked at him as though she were trying to understand him.

He liked that she tried to understand him.

"It's near the door. I didn't want to get caught." Cruz cursed himself for not having stayed another night at Trini's. He had known he was risking meeting Isola. She's nice, he thought, and gorgeous.

"Maybe we can talk while I pack up the house," Isola said. "Did you know I was coming?"

"No. I need to leave soon." He looked at the clock, then the door. She seemed so much like her mother, but Cruz remembered Marina's words, "I can't rely on her. My daughter doesn't like to help." He wanted to keep his promise. But the daughter wasn't going to stop asking questions until she knew everything. "Thank you for not calling the police."

"It's nothing." Isola sipped her coffee. She seemed to be thinking hard, as though contemplating the existence of shrimp, as Marina often said. "You scared me a little. But I was exhausted. When I got in all I wanted was sleep."

"Sí," Cruz said, almost to himself. Sleep was all he had wanted when he sneaked back into Marina's house earlier.

Outside orange plumes cut across the blue-violet sky. It was time to go find work and another place to sleep. "I have to go." He washed his cup in the sink and rolled his blanket.

"Can't you stay longer?" Isola tilted her head. Her voice sounded as though she were singing her words.

Cruz thought she looked as though she might cry. "I am sorry about your mother," he said. "I wish we could have met earlier, in happier times." Cruz picked up his things and turned toward the door.

"Wait," she said. "I could use some help packing up the house." She met him at the door.

Cruz listened to what she said. How could he leave her begging him for his help? He convinced himself to stay and help Marina's daughter. Apparently, she had no one else. He promised himself he would respect Marina's wishes and leave after he had helped her. It wasn't too much to ask.

"You're not bothered by not knowing me?" Cruz said.

"I don't know why, but I trust you."

"Bueno," he said. From the look of her sad catlike eyes, he knew she trusted everybody she met. He put down his things and waited for her to tell him what she needed done.

9

Isola made a quick tour of the house. Cruz followed her and tried to understand what she wanted him to do. He noticed new things in the house, a box of books, luggage, and Isola's purse. After going out to the backyard and checking all the rooms, they sat down in the kitchen again.

"There are so many boxes and drawers to go through. Can you come back in a few days after I figure out a plan?"

Cruz nodded. Pobrecita, she really needs help, he thought. She's different from her mother, strong on the outside, but very hurt. "Sad" was the word he thought described Isola best.

"Thank you for offering to help. I could really use it. Look at all these boxes. So, you'll come . . ." Isola clasped her hands to her heart and rested her chin on her fingers. She seemed to be calculating and thinking very hard.

"Wednesday." Cruz finished her thoughts. He was happy to see her smile. He bowed slightly, grabbed his bag, and walked toward the bus stop.

2

Mother's Words

Nothing about her mother's desert house reminded her of her childhood home. In San Francisco, the family's painted lady, with its lattice trim, crown moldings, and rich mahogany furniture, had exuded a personality all its own and was much more than a mere house. The walls had witnessed Isola's triumphs and failures and she had felt comforted by the charm of her mother's whimsical décor. Family photos scaled the hallway wall leading upstairs. There was a photo of Isola as a baby and several others of her grandparents and her aunt Bernarda's children wearing Isola's old clothes. However, most of the large and small framed pictures were of her parents' wedding day.

The new house in Arizona was a mystery, as puzzling as the woman her mother had become. The only familiar sight in the room was her mother's collection of perfume bottles. Her father had brought the colorful decanters from his rare assignments abroad. The smallest one, an iridescent blue, had been Mom's favorite. Isola opened the bottle. A whiff of lotus blossom and lavender and she was a child again, sitting patiently as her mother brushed her hair, enjoying the rare undivided attention. Isola doubted her mother had worn the delicate perfume in her new life in Arizona.

The doorbell and several knocks jarred Isola back to the room filled with stale air and a ribbon of childhood fragrances. How she regretted their lack of closeness and the lost years of her mother's desert days. Who had she become? The doorbell. Had Cruz returned? She'd better make herself decent.

She slipped on a sundress from her mother's closet, ran back down, and opened the door. The sun's white light made the day feel much later than

7:30 in the morning. A woman with light brown eyes and dark weathered skin stood next to a young man who stared down at his tennis shoes while he scuffed quartz rocks on the walkway.

"Señorita Isola?" The lady smiled and pointed to Isola's dress.

"Yes?"

"I have a picture of doña Marina in that flowered dress. Cómo se parecen. You're twins."

"People always tell us that." Isola waited for the woman to say what she wanted.

"I'm Josefina Jiménez. This is my nephew Alfonso." The youth with the slicked-back hair lifted his head. Josefina wore a black uniform with her name stitched on it in cursive letters. "Your mother loved that dress."

"It's comfortable. You knew my mother well?"

The woman nodded.

Another one. Isola regretted answering the door. She was never going to get anything done if people who knew her mother kept dropping in. On the other hand, she might learn something useful. Be patient, she reminded herself.

"Come in." Isola offered them the couch and pulled up a chair from the kitchen.

"Your mother taught me English here." She pointed to the sparsely furnished living room. "In the garage, there are chairs for the classes and uh, em." She drew letters in the air.

"Chalkboard?"

"Sí. Chalkboard," Josefina carefully repeated.

"I was wondering about that," Isola said, not meaning to share that thought with Josefina. The house felt strangely cold and unlived in, maybe because it was used as a classroom. Where had her mother stashed the photos of her wedding she had once treasured? Her mother had looked carefree, barefoot in a white dress and flowers in her hair.

"¿Cómo?"

"Never mind. Do you want some water?"

"No, gracias. You teach classes too, right?

"College literature. Not the same kind of classes my mother taught. Her job's much harder."

Josefina nodded as if lost in her own thoughts. Her nephew fidgeted in his seat and adjusted the spidery hairnet over his long sideburns. The kid looked both young and tough. Loops of tattooed letters peeked out from his crisp sleeves. Alfonso gave Isola an apologetic look before rising to shuffle past them into the bathroom. He knew where the bathroom was. Isola wondered if Josefina wanted her to teach them classes. She wasn't planning on picking up where her mother had left off.

Josefina scooted closer to Isola. She was obviously waiting for her nephew to leave the room.

"I hate to bother you, Señorita Isola, pero, did Marina leave an envelope for me?" She uncrossed fit, stocky legs. Isola suspected she was younger than her weathered face suggested.

"An envelope? I haven't seen anything, but I got in late last night. You know more than I do. Do you have an idea where the envelope might be?"

"No, I'm sorry. I should not bother you." Josefina stood and fished a paper out of her purse.

"It's OK. Leave me your phone number and I'll call you if I see anything."

"Do you know what's in the envelope?"

"It's a mica para Alfonso." She seemed anxious as though she wanted to ask Isola for money.

"What's a mica?"

"Papers. A card for work."

"Oh, right." Isola hadn't heard the word mentioned in years, decades. The people her mother had taught often worried about getting a mica for work. "Your nephew seems too young. He should be in school."

"He already finish school in México."

Isola was too tired to argue with her. She was familiar with the scenario, a boy who should be in school but worked to help his family.

"I'll get back to you if I find it."

"Gracias." Josefina scribbled on a paper from her purse.

"Can you describe the mica? What does the card say? Does it have your nephew's name on it?"

Josefina's mouth twisted in a downward curve. She checked her watch and took a deep breath. "Doña Marina say I can have your father's social security card. I wasn't going to bother you, but I had to ask for Alfonso."

As if on cue, Alfonso came out of the bathroom. His aunt motioned him outside. She thrust the paper in Isola's hand, pointed to the door, and mumbled something about not wanting to be late.

"I've never seen my father's social security card. I can't believe you want it for your nephew." Isola choked her words out. She knew the social security card was just a piece of paper, but she felt as if the woman was asking her to dig up her father's remains.

"I didn't mean to upset you. You . . ."

"You must be mistaken. There's no way Mother would've told you that." Isola turned away and squeezed her throbbing forehead.

"I'm sorry. I shouldn't have come." Josefina closed the door behind her.

First the missing wedding photos, and now this woman wanted to borrow her father's identity. She regretted not bringing Renée or Gretchen, even Jeremy, somebody, anybody that knew her parents. Isola's head felt heavy and hot "like water for chocolate," the Mexican saying went. She crushed the piece of paper with Josefina's phone number on it and threw the wad at the wall. Gretchen was right. This was too much for her to handle on her own. No, she had to pull herself together. She was a grown girl, a professor, no less, capable of taking care of her mother's affairs. So stop crying, she told herself. She was still sobbing in the empty room when she heard the car screech away from the driveway. Was this woman telling the truth? Isola didn't know what to think, and worse, she was upset with her mother all over again. Wasn't anything sacred to Marina? She had some nerve! Isola didn't doubt that if she herself were dead, her mother wouldn't have wasted any time in giving away her identity. Marina had given away everything Isola had ever owned as a child, her old clothes and shoes. She had even sent Isola's favorite toys to her cousins in México. "I thought you had outgrown toys," her mother would say in her defense of charity. Isola was determined to find her father's documents, but she wasn't going to hand them over to Josefina or Alfonso or anyone.

3
Daddy's Home

San Francisco, California, 1981

The screech of her father's car grew louder. As it revved up, the engine sounded as if it were complaining; it didn't follow her mother's "no whining" policy. The car ceased its wail and Isola raced around the living room and collected books and games she had forgotten to put away. Her mother had taught her to clean up after herself, especially when she or her father came home. "We work too hard to pick up after la pequeña señorita," her mother often said. It didn't take Isola long to realize that her parents were in a better mood and tolerated her forgetting other chores when the house was tidy. Isola plopped onto the couch and tried to look cool and relaxed and not like the frantic Tasmanian devil she had turned into minutes ago.

Isola welcomed her father with arms stretched out, ready for him to lift her off the ground. She was too big to play elephant's trunk and have him swing her from side to side as they both made jungle noises. He squeezed and kissed her and his moustache tickled her face. She rubbed her nose and cheek against his fuzzy stubble.

"How's my little secretary doing?" he said.

"Ready to work." Isola gave him a military salute.

"Where's Mami?"

"At a meeting. Mrs. Sánchez is home." Isola pulled her unhappy duckbill pout, pretended to sound hurt and annoyed. Technically, Mrs. Sánchez was babysitting her, but Isola didn't mind being alone in the house. Isola knew to dial Mrs. Sánchez's number if anyone other than her parents, rang the doorbell. Even if someone she knew from Glen Park or from her mother's school dropped by, she was on strict orders to be chaperoned by her caretaker, who lived in the garage apartment behind their house. However, no one ever came to her house in the Mission District, which was fine because Isola was a bit ashamed of the state it was in. Her mother had said that their house was a "fixer-upper," but they didn't have the money to fix it up. Sometimes her mother dropped her off at Gretchen's house and the two would practice German words. Isola enjoyed spending time with her mother's old friend, but she preferred days when she was allowed to stay at home and wait for her father. Most days her father worked late and rarely came home before she fell asleep. Hearing his voice was a treat better than candy.

"Mom said to tell you there's chili."

"¿Chile? ¿De veras?" Her father extended the "eh" in chile and rolled his r. Late at night when he was tired, he always spoke Spanish, which made his voice sound like a carrousel—musical and fun. Isola understood everything, but answered in English. Too much work to search for the correct word.

"Yes, there's chili. But can we have McDonald's? Just some fries, maybe? It doesn't have to be a whole Happy Meal," she pleaded on her tiptoes.

"You mean McDonald's as in the golden arches?" He repeated their private joke.

"No. I don't mean McDonald's as in the golden arches." Isola no longer enjoyed their game.

"You seem happy already so you don't need a Happy Meal when you've got Mami's chile."

"Leftover chile." Isola pronounced "left," as if she could throw the soiled word into the washing machine. "Daddy. You know I mean McDonald's as in the golden arches." She used her sweetest voice and tickled his sides. "Do I smell french fries?"

"Perhaps the golden arches have come to you?" He walked to his favorite chair and lifted his briefcase.

"I knew it!" Isola did a little dance around the living room, twirling in circles, avoiding the square edges of the coffee table. Her father jiggled a sack from McDonald's. Isola reached for the bag. The fries were still warm.

"Did you bring proofs?" Isola preferred checking her father's articles for spelling errors to doing her homework. She delighted in seeing what would go into the paper before anyone else did. She also collected her father's tear sheets. Sometimes she'd reread his articles, especially when she didn't understand and was too embarrassed to ask someone to explain them to her. She wanted her parents to believe she was a "big girl" who understood everything, and not a whiny eight-year-old like Sarah, the girl from school who cried about everything, even a lost pencil.

"Yes. I'll put you to work after you eat, mija."

She gave her father another hug. "McDonald's is ten times better than leftover chile."

"I'm going to have your mami's chile."

"Is that why you didn't want McDonald's? Because you're going to eat *chi-leh*?"

"I don't think so, mija. I had a big lunch." He patted his stomach. "I'll save this for later or you can eat these cookies."

"Cookies? You tricked me."

He shrugged his shoulders and pulled out an unopened package of post-it notes. She loved the little gifts he brought her.

"More gifts? Time to work."

"Time to get ready for bed."

4

Cobwebs

Chandler, Arizona, 1997

Too many things seemed unreal and Isola didn't know what to make of Josefina or her mother's promise of the mica or even the classroom. She wanted to dismiss Josefina's claims, but the chairs and the chalkboard in the large closet near the garage convinced her there was some truth to Josefina's words.

Boxes spilled out of the corners of the garage. Most contained stacks of old and moldy papers full of squished bugs. Isola hated the thought of unpacking all those boxes. But it was the only way to get to her father's documents. After an exhaustive search, she found several file folders for her mother's students, but nothing for Josefina or Cruz. She tried her luck upstairs in her mother's bedroom, where there were even more boxes, plastic file cabinets, her mother's desk, and an oak wardrobe.

Her mother was more organized than she had ever been when Isola was a child. In her new life, Marina had alphabetical files on everyone she knew—even people she didn't know but wanted to meet. One folder chronicled Marina's near-miss with President Clinton. "Not close enough to shake his hand. Handsome in person." Her mother had scribbled on a pink sticky note stapled to a clipping of Clinton's visit to Arizona State University.

The file with Isola's name on it contained a few photos of herself as a young child, dressing up in her mother's tie-dyed creations. Isola had noticed a couple of those old dresses in Marina's closet, but didn't register them as being the same ones until she saw the old photograph. Marina had been ruthlessly generous in giving away her daughter's clothes and strangely sentimental about keeping her own outdated styles. Isola's file, stuffed with postcards she and her mother had exchanged over their less-than-communicative years, was the thickest one she'd opened so far. Her postcards with their boring and cryptic words chronicled the extent to which her mother pretended they had a normal relationship. Isola now wished she had written more than a few scribbles.

She wondered what had happened to the long letter she had sent to her mother after hearing she was ill. She had written several tear-stained drafts of her sorrow and apology which ended up charred on the gas stove. The final computer version seemed to have lost the sincerity of her earlier drafts. Had her mother realized how genuine her remorse had been? Isola felt crummy and small at not finding the letter she had struggled over, but reminded herself that it was pointless to try to reconstruct her mother's life from the dozens of boxes she left. If the situation were reversed, her mother would be just as baffled about the infant who had grown up to be so different from her. Isola was convinced her mother had been the one who had shape-shifted into another being. When she saw women glowing with maternal pride in their grown daughters, clinging and caressing them in public, she envied their closeness. They were like clouds, the same but different. She spied them at malls and museums, studied the contours of their faces, noting each resemblance and how easily they communicated with each other, both silently and verbally. She sometimes had to concentrate hard just to remember the details of her own mother's face.

Isola reminded herself to stay focused and not daydream as she rummaged through her mother's dresser. The search for her father's papers exposed an unexpected treasure, her mother's diamond ring. As a child, Isola had always been fascinated with it. During the few minutes her mother would let her hold the ring and play with it, she'd remind Isola that the diamond had been abuelita Angelina's only possession. Isola never met her grandmother Angelina, but envisioned a grand lady with a slender figure, a princess worthy of the delicate gem.

"Mamá never had a house, but your abuelo Juan José bought her a diamond." Isola remembered the story well. She followed the beams of sparkles around the room, the way she did when she was a child. The ring had to be one of her mother's most valuable possessions. None of the lawyers had mentioned it in her mother's probate papers. When she didn't see the diamond on her finger at the hospital, she'd assumed Marina had lost it. Isola hadn't dared ask her mother about it. The ring had been partly responsible for their estrangement. Magic faded from the starlit room and she felt a cold shame chill her body as she remembered thinking her mother had purposely kept her grandmother's ring for herself. The old guilt curse knotted her stomach. Marina had done so much to restore her father's inheritance. It was never about money, only about their stupid pride.

San Franciso, California 1993

Jeremy's blond locks in the sliver of sunlight made him look like a martyred saint. In high school, when she had first met him, Isola was attracted to his dirty, disheveled hair. Even more thrilling was the moment she discovered that his hair wasn't dirty at all, but exuded the crisp smell of baby shampoo. Jeremy was her cherub when he wasn't complaining; he was also good at fixing her computer whenever the machine developed a mind of its own.

He jostled his game console. His body swayed and jumped as he defeated aliens. Isola knew not to disturb him during his Doom game sessions, but she had made up her mind to confront her mother and needed Jeremy's help this morning.

Isola stalked around the room and waved her arms. Jeremy continued to follow the action on his computer screen. He had a talent for shutting her out whenever he set aside time for defending the world.

She put her face in front of the screen.

"Move your head!" He shifted left. He was still in the game. "Yes!" he rejoiced and continued to sway as he evaded aliens jumping out of dark corners.

"Jeremy, I need to talk to you." She pulled up a chair next to him and fluttered her hands by his ears. He ignored her.

She parted the purple velveteen curtains she had hung up in his "office," shedding light on musty objects that were in desperate need of airing.

20

He shielded his eyes at the blinding light and crouched closer to the computer screen. "Oooh, no, shit!" he wailed, slamming the joystick hard on his desk.

"Do you have to be so dramatic? It's only a game."

"What the hell, Izzy? It's my day off." His cherub face puckered into a demonic gaze.

"I need to ask for a favor. I need your help." Isola tried to make herself small and cute. He only called her "Izzy" when he was mad at her. She objected to "Izzy"; it wasn't her at all, but Jeremy persisted with the nickname.

"Don't you think I have needs, too?" He looked her straight in the eye.

"I'm not trying to piss you off." She kept her eyes downcast.

"Whatever." He pointed pitifully to his computer screen as though Isola had taken away everything he had in the world.

"I'm sorry, but I had to get your attention now."

"What is it? I'm listening," he said, flipping through last week's issue of *Technology*.

"I'm ready to talk to my mother about my inheritance." She omitted mentioning her father. Jeremy had run out of patience for her dead father after their graduation from high school.

His bored, glazed face showed no sympathy. "Why do you have to bug me? Go talk to her."

"But . . ."

"It's not my problem, not my money."

"She's easier to deal with when you're around. Walk over there with me. You can leave before we get into it. Don't forget I helped you with your sister."

"Yeah, but that was different." He swooshed his head so that his hair fell over his eyes, the signal that meant he no longer wanted to talk.

"Come on. With you it's *mijo* this, *mijo* that, all politeness and civility. She'll be more difficult if I go alone." She clasped her hands to her chest.

He exhaled his heavy, dragonlike sigh, but Isola didn't mind the huffy protest as long as he agreed to go with her. He flicked his bangs away from his eyes.

"Thank you, thank you." She kissed his cheek to seal the deal. She gathered her purse and keys and closed his curtains.

"OK, but you owe me," he said. "Soon as it gets ugly, I'm out of there." He slipped on his unlaced tennis shoes. Isola gave him a salute, then smiled. He was her saint again.

The walk to her mother's from Jeremy's was manageable, only a short jog down 24th Street, across Church to Dolores. However, Isola asked Jeremy to drive them instead. She didn't want to be winded for the big talk with her mother. They soon arrived at the beautiful Victorian her parents had fixed up with money they had received from Grandma Palan in Poland. Jeremy tried the doorbell. Isola heard Lola Beltrán's voice belt out the sad songs her mother loved to play over and over. She turned the knob. Her mother never locked her door, said it was impolite.

The nose-curling smells of her childhood overtook her. Her mother was making tomatillo salsa. The strong whiff of hot chiles suggested her mother was preparing her famous spicy salsa that proved how Mexican she was and how wimpy Isola was. Isola's eyes watered from the boiled jalapeños peppering the air. She sneezed and daubed the corners of her eyes with her sweater.

"Pásale, don't stand there. I knew it was you." Her mother urged them in. She wore the old yellow apron she refused to throw away.

"Always claiming to be psychic," Isola murmured to Jeremy. Jeremy put his finger to his lip.

"I have hojarascas and some fresh tortillas and some other little antojitos."

"Cookies and homemade tortillas? Who is this really for? You know I gave up lard ten years ago?" Isola flinched from Jeremy's warning pinch at the soft skin at the crook of her elbow. She knew she wasn't off to a great start, but her mother had that effect on her, turned her into a rebellious little brat. This wasn't working. "You never cook. What's all this baking about?"

"I'm cooking, aren't I?"

"Now you are, but you never made all this stuff for me," Isola answered, but her mother was no longer standing in the doorway. She was busy setting the table and offering Jeremy a plate.

"I know mijo wants a tortilla with some beans and melted queso." Her voice sang with delight.

Jeremy smiled and took his place of honor in the kitchen. The two carried on in Spanish. Isola's mother didn't seem to mind Jeremy's Cuban accent and the funny way he spoke Spanish as though he had an olive pit tucked under his tongue.

You don't have to be psychic to know a twenty-year-old boy will eat anything. Isola rolled her eyes. Jeremy was like a puppy in her mother's kitchen waiting for treats and attention. Why did I bring him? She retreated to the living room and plunked down on the worn, soft couch that had lost all its bounce. She took off her shoes to prop her feet up, but the oak coffee table was littered with real estate pamphlets and newspaper ads. She read some of the papers. The cassette player clicked off and Isola enjoyed the silence. She closed her eyes for a few seconds and then went back to studying the pamphlets.

"Mom! What's all this?" She picked up three flyers and walked toward the kitchen.

Jeremy finished sopping up the beans and salsa on his plate with the last corner of his tortilla. He never failed to remind Isola of how much he loved the fiery kick of her mother's tomatillo salsa. He put his plate in the sink. Her mother caressed his cheek. He smiled and thanked her before stretching out on the couch in the living room.

"My work is done here. I'm moving to Arizona." Her mother gathered pots and dishes and put them in the sink.

Her work. Being a self-imposed busybody and campaign groupie was a job well suited to her mother, who worked for free, but Isola was surprised to hear her mother say *her work* was done.

"Arizona? When were you going to tell me?" Isola sat down at the kitchen table.

"Since when do you concern yourself with my affairs? You who study dead white people." Her mother sang the last three words. She laughed. Jeremy echoed her laughter from the living room.

"Don't you think your moving is something I should know about?"

"When the time is right, I'll tell you."

"You always say that. I'm not going to argue about this. This is a good time for me to get my money that Dad left me."

"How many times, Isola? ¡Por fin! Papi didn't want you to have the money until you're thirty."

"Why are you making me wait forever?"

"Forever is a long time. You only have to wait ten years."

"I was a kid when he died. He worried I'd spend the money on toys and frivolous things."

"And why do you need the money so badly?" Her mother gathered the steaming skins of chili peppers and tomatillos and threw them into the trash can.

"I want to buy a house," Isola said.

"Real estate is expensive in San Francisco." Her mother dried her hands on her apron.

"That's my point." Isola took a taste of the hojarasca. The small bite turned into more nibbles until she had polished off the whole cookie. She washed it down with coffee her mother placed before her. Lard cookies were irrestible. She dusted off the cinnamon and sugar from her hands and blouse. "No more cookies." She hadn't meant to vocalize the thought. The coffee was sweet and had a hint of cinnamon.

"Bebita, you have a good deal at Gretchen's. The best apartment, the best view, and the nice furniture she doesn't charge you for. She could charge a lot more money for that apartment."

Isola rolled her eyes at her mother calling her "Bebita." "Gretchen's always spying on me. I might as well be living here," Isola said.

"If she opens your mail, it's because you're negligent." Her mother's strange smile turned into a small burst of laughter.

"So you heard about her opening my mail. It's not funny, Mom."

Her mother shrugged her shoulders.

"Gretchen's only looking out for you," her mother said.

"I don't need her to look out for me. Opening my mail is not right."

"I don't know the details. If you no longer want to live there, this is your house; you can move back any time."

"I thought you were selling the house," Isola said.

"If you want to collect your money early, you can buy this house and maybe give something to your cousin Bertha. Her kids can't afford school uniforms. You should also think about sponsoring Manuelita."

Isola remained silent. When her mother turned, Isola saw how serious she was. Her mother wasn't kidding. "I'm supposed to pay you for the house and give money to Bertha because her only talent is having kids she can't afford? Eight of them and counting." Isola heard her voice rise to decibels she hadn't reached in years.

"Isola, don't bark at me." Her mother's voice sounded like she was scolding her in Spanish, but Isola was familiar with the English words that were meant to end all conversation.

"I'm not barking. You've always put them before me. If you care so much about your relatives, why don't *you* help them?"

"I do help my family," she said. Her mother put her face close to Isola's. "Who else is going to help? You? Who parades around in a new outfit every day?"

"What? Just because you haven't bought yourself anything new since Dad died doesn't mean I spend all my money on clothes."

Her mother's face became dark and constricted. She looked as though she had stopped breathing. The pink returned to her brown cheeks. "Are *you* calling *me* a liar?"

"Papi was the only one who cared about me and he's dead. You never cared about me or him, just everyone else."

"You . . . I . . ." her mother said. She swallowed several times, but was incapable of saying any more.

She heard the thwack of her mother's hand slapping her straight across her face, then felt the throb. Her mother's diamond ring caught on the edge of Isola's lip. Isola's tongue reached for the blood oozing out of the corner of her mouth. Her mother had never hit her. She clasped her hand to her lip and held the warm spot on her face as though keeping the left side of her jaw from falling off. Her mother stared at her coldly as though looking at a stranger.

"At my age, I should have a house full of grandchildren, like your tía Alicia." Her mother continued speaking in a Spanish that sounded like gibberish. Isola recognized the words *malcriada, malagradecida,* and *maldita,* her mother's various translations for ungrateful, rotten little girl.

Jeremy walked in. He seemed surprise to see blood on Isola's face. He took step toward her and hesitated before speaking. "I think I'll just . . ."

"Leave!" Isola and her mother yelled at the same time. Jeremy turned his back on them and waved.

"Wait!" Isola yelled for him to stop. "I'm coming too."

She turned to her mother. "Forget it. I'm not taking my money." Isola ran out the door and caught up with Jeremy.

Jeremy dabbed her lip with the bottom of his shirt. He gently grasped her shoulders as he examined her bleeding lip. "I might have a Band-Aid in the car."

"Leave it," she said, "it's nothing."

As they walked toward Jeremy's car, Isola noticed another car pull in near her mother's house. Isola watched as four people got out and went to her mother's door, where they were greeted with hugs and kisses. When it came to spending time with her friends, her mother was always quick at recovering from fights. Without the ratty apron, she looked beautiful and carefree, like the young woman she once was when Isola's father was still alive. Isola longed for her mother to open her arms and heart and welcome her with the same inviting face she now showed her friends.

5

Sometimes a
Phone Call . . .

Chandler, Arizona, 1999

Isola licked her finger and dusted off the framed photograph of herself and Jeremy. He was another casualty of her talent for messy endings. Her life was a story of burnt bridges and no returns. She forgave her father. She could never stay mad at him for anything. He was simply walking, minding his own business, when the car killed him. Her mother, on the other hand, was someone who, against all advice and with a history of skin cancer, had moved to the desert. Isola grew frustrated and felt helpless all over again. The argument about her father's money was an easy excuse for both of them to ignore each other and grow apart, but her mother should have been big enough to apologize first. At least she looked happy in the photograph with Jeremy, innocent and sweet, before she had stopped believing in fairytales and love. She remembered the long purple dress, purple tights (it was her purple phase) and the faux-fur coat that blended with her then-long brown hair. She looked like an adoring child, gazing up at Jeremy and dwarfed by his long legs. She not only recalled the time and place of the photograph, but also remembered the stranger who had taken the picture ten years ago. Yet lately, she had a hard time remembering the map of Jeremy's body. She once had memorized every pore on Jeremy's big nose and eggshell skin, the contours of his porcelain back, and the blond hairs on his legs, his chicken sticks, she'd tease.

The Cuban often passed as white. She laughed and remembered all the times he had surprised people by speaking his Cuban Spanish with his quick-fire accent. They both enjoyed their private game. People never knew what to make of Isola, who was often told how exotic she looked. She was often mistaken for Thai or Filipino, but usually people guessed she was Mexican by her dark skin.

Her mother often joked about her daughter's gringo boyfriend. "Cubanos are not the same as Chicanos!" her mother argued with Jeremy. Her scratchy laughter made the three of them smile. Her little jabs were in jest. With Jeremy, it was always, "*mijo* this, *mijo* that, where's my son-in-law, when's the wedding?" and on and on. Her mother should've dated him, Isola thought. When Isola told her about their breakup, her mother didn't want to hear about how selfish and cruel Jeremy had been, but cried as if she were losing the son she had always wanted. Where was Saint Jeremy when her mother had died? He sent two lousy flower arrangements to the church services and burial. *My condolences*, the card had read. Condolences! Isola struggled to stay focused and not allow herself to spin madly into rage. We were over ages ago. He doesn't owe me anything. She was deep in her old pattern of Jeremy disgust when her cell phone's loud ring startled her. She ran up the stairs and caught her breath.

"Renée. I can't believe it."

"Are we still doing lunch?"

"Lunch?" Isola smiled at the warmth in Renée's rich honeyed voice. "I can't. I'm in Arizona."

"I thought you were waiting till after the summer."

"I was, but I changed my mind."

"Do you always have to be so impulsive? I said I'd help you, but I can't leave now," Renée said.

"It's done. I'm in her house. I had to get it over with. And it's a jumbled mess. I can't find anything."

"Gretchen said you were over there, but I didn't believe her. She gave me the number and I left a few messages." Renée sounded hurt.

It's just lunch, Isola thought. "I haven't checked the messages on the home number yet, but that's a good idea." Isola sat down. She sensed she was in for a long Rénee heart-to-heart.

"What about your fellowship?" Renée sounded as though she were still scolding her.

"It's OK. I postponed it." Isola said.

"You can do that?"

"Yes. Mourning seems to be an official American disability."

"A little humor is good. If it weren't for my new job I'd . . ."

"Don't worry. I'm fine. I'll pack up this place in one, two, three weeks tops." Isola knew Renée would come if she really needed her.

"Why don't you get Jeremy to help you?"

"Puh-leeze. My life didn't end when I broke up with him." Isola laughed.

"What's so funny, then?"

"My mother has a picture of him, of us."

Isola tried to think of something to break the silence. Renée, like her mother, had a hard time imagining Isola happy without Jeremy by her side. Isola knew that leaving that childish relationship was one of the best things she had done for herself.

"I got into the public health program." Renée finally broke the heavy silence.

"That's great." Isola wanted to summon the enthusiasm of their sonic, high-pitched screams from high school; but only managed a mousy "Congratulations."

"I owe you some thanks, Ms. Ph.D."

"Shut up. You don't owe me anything."

"Can't you just say 'you're welcome'?"

"Sorry, I'm happy for you. We'll celebrate when I get back."

"You need to get Jeremy to help you. It's not like he's busy or anything, Mr. Uncle left him shitloads of bank."

"It's complicated. He has a new girlfriend."

"After all you did for that fool's dog? To the very end when that crippled animal died."

"I know. Poor Trolley," Isola whispered. She loved dogs and Trolley was more like their child. The cocker spaniel had become fiercely loyal to her, even though he had been Jeremy's dog before she had met him. Someday she'd replace Jeremy, but Trolley was irreplacable. She vowed never to adopt another red cocker spaniel like her faithful Trolley, who had collapsed at her feet before taking his last breath.

"Who cares about Jeremy?" She could hear Renée's annoyed tone.

"He called once to see if I'd agree to meet Carola. Apparently she's paranoid because we dated for so long."

"Carola, like the car? What a freak. I hope you said no."

Isola smiled. She didn't bother explaining that her name was spelled differently than the car. Renée knew how to be supportive, even though she was wild about Jeremy. "I didn't want to meet her, or see him."

"You helped his sister get amnesty in Florida. And he won't do a thing for you? I swear!"

"He didn't even come to the funeral. Remember?"

"But . . ."

"Forget it. I don't need any help, really."

"But if it was his mother, you'd drop everything for him."

"No. That's not true. Not anymore."

"Whatever."

Isola heard more tongue clicking and cheek sucking from Renée. "Yeah, whatever." Isola didn't have the energy to shout a bad-assed "whatevuh" back to Renée.

"Why don't you have yourself a new man?"

"I've been busy the last four years. After you start your doctoral program, I'll be sure to ask you about your social life, Miss-solve-the-ills-of-the-world-Doctor."

"Mmmm, mmm. You don't have to get all toxic on me."

"Sorry, I have to go. Sorry about lunch too. Maybe in a couple weeks."

"'Kay. Call if you need anything. And stop getting toxic on people."

Renée hung up.

Isola didn't care that Renée always had to have the last word in every conversation they'd had since high school.

She searched for a small box. She decided to take all the framed photos back to San Franciso, including the one of her and Jeremy. Not because she still had feelings for him, but because it was part of her history. Maybe Renée was right. Maybe she needed help, big time.

Stay focused, she reminded herself. "Sí se puede." She whispered her mother's old mantra. She needed to work quickly without anyone else, especially Jeremy, weighing her down, but she was tired after emptying only one kitchen cabinet. She hoped that was the worst of it. She sat and watched the dust filter through the window like alien angels come to comfort her.

Her mother's desert dealings, whether running a school or a safe house, remained a mystery. Isola continued to feel like a stranger as she rummaged through her mother's secrets. She should have been prepared for the sight of her mother's jail release forms, given that her childhood was filled with being dragged to political campaigns and protests. That her mother had been in an Arizona jail wasn't as shocking as the fact that she hadn't called Isola for bail or held it over her like the drama queen she knew her to be. Her mother had a talent for making her feel guilty, especially when she had no way of being at fault. Who was she relying on for help? Isola acknowledged the fact that they didn't have the kind of supportive relationship in which they could confide in each other and was even willing to take some of the blame for her mother choosing the desert's isolation. If only you had given me a little more credit, Mom. Isola sifted through her mother's prison release papers. She stared at the forms, as if expecting the pages to start speaking the story of why her mother had been arrested. Isola had no trouble picturing her mother selflessly doing time without complaining or telling anyone. She guessed it had something to do with her mother's radar for lost political causes. Why couldn't you trust me with this one?

There was no end in sight to the tucked-away pieces of her mother's life. She sat on the carpet and took a short break from the files. From the floor's vantage, Isola saw her mother's handbag tucked between the bed and the nightstand. Its metal clasp shimmered, as if vibrating with an energy all its own. The contents of the purse distracted her from the futile search for her father's file. The purse did not contain his identification, as she had hoped, but instead she found an airline ticket tucked next to her mother's checkbook. The flight to San Francisco was scheduled for two weeks after Marina's death. A tornado of mixed emotions swirled inside Isola's gut. She was elated one minute, ashamed and depressed the next. She tugged at the short strands of her bob and scratched at the stubbly spot at the nape of her neck. She actually was coming to visit me. Don't cry. This will only be harder if you start crying. She took a deep breath.

Isola didn't have any direct proof, but she was willing to bet that Gretchen knew of her mother's intention to visit and it would explain Gretchen's recent erratic behavior. Gretchen had been acting funny before her mother fell ill. Two months had passed since Gretchen had complained about Isola's late rent payment, but she had kept coming up with excuses to fix her apartment and tend to doors and appliances Isola had stopped using on account of Gretchen's neglect. Gretchen loved playing detective. All this time, I thought she was being a senile busybody. As her landlady, Gretchen had the power to ensure her mother's visit was a big surprise. Isola thought it was like her mother to warn her best friend about the visit, and not her daughter. Gretchen, to her credit, kept secrets better than anyone. She had managed to throw a surprise party for Isola's eighth birthday, while keeping it a secret from Isola and her parents. It wasn't such a big stretch to believe Gretchen was in on her mother's plans. Isola only wished Gretchen had let *her* in on it.

Hours passed and still no sign of her father's documents or an envelope for Josefina or a file for either of them. During her encounter with Josefina, Isola had received a voice mail about a potential buyer for the house. She was crazy to think she could resolve and pack up all of her mother's mysteries by the end of the week. So little about her mother's last years made any sense. It was bad enough that the house seemed as though someone or several persons had relieved it of its furniture and valuables. She suspected Cruz and Josefina, but quickly exonerated Cruz on account of his kind eyes and the fact he hadn't asked her for anything. But maybe that's why he hadn't asked. Had he already helped himself to the house? Her instinct told her she could trust Cruz if he came back on Wednesday. She believed he was an honest, trustworthy man. She wasn't so sure about Josefina and the nephew.

6

Wednesday

A scraping sound like someone burying a dead body in the backyard woke her up. A bad dream, Isola thought, or a scenario from one of the horror movies Jeremy used to force her to watch. She rubbed sleep from her eyes and looked out the upstairs window. Below, a man appeared to be digging or gardening. She remembered it was Wednesday, the day Cruz was supposed to help her pack up the house. Apparently he had gotten an early start and was yanking weeds from flower beds around the swimming pool and trimming the sprawling, overgrown bougainvillea. He had already transformed the neglected yard into an oasis. His shirt was off and Isola watched the sweat run down his biceps. He was a working man, she thought, with real muscles, so different from Jeremy's delicate and pale arms. Four years and I'm still comparing men to Jeremy. What's wrong with me? Isola remembered her manners, brushed her teeth, dressed, and ran downstairs.

"Thank you, but you don't have to do all that."

"Discúlpame. No quería molestarte." Cruz seemed worried.

"Are you kidding? You're not bothering me, but I only needed help with some boxes for Goodwill and hauling the junk and large trash."

Cruz had a proud look on his face. "I know where to take all boxes and extra trash," he said.

"How long have you been here? The yard looks great."

"Early, since 5:30. I knocked on the back door, but you were sleeping. If I hadn't dropped the shovel, you would not have noticed me."

Cruz dunked his bandana in the pool and wiped his chest and face before putting his shirt back on. "I'm almost finished, then we can do the boxes."

"OK, but first we'll have breakfast."

"Gracias." Cruz nodded.

Cruz sat at the same place and used the yellow cup Isola had given him the first time they had met two days ago. Today he seemed at ease, at home, almost. She served him scrambled eggs, bagels, and cream cheese. He ate the eggs quickly, but examined the bagel, turning it over, as if it were a miniature spaceship. Isola sliced it for him and spread a generous dollop of cream cheese on one side. Cruz ate it and closed his eyes. He rubbed his belly. She laughed at his expression of gratitude. She was the one who was grateful for having someone to help her. She would have served him steak and eggs if she had thought of it. No one else had come to her rescue.

"Did you do a lot of gardening for my mother?"

"I worked different jobs for her. I owe her my life." Cruz spoke the words without flinching.

"You never said that before." Isola looked at him. She wondered what else he hadn't mentioned.

"Doña Marina was working with Rescate Ángeles. She found me in the desert. I needed water and was lost, disoriented. I had tried to cross before, but got caught."

"What's Rescate? Rescue Angels?"

"Yes. They're a group that help us when the coyotes abandon us in the desert."

"I'm sorry. I'm an idiot stuck in my own little bubble. I think I've heard of them, but I didn't know my mother was a member."

Cruz laughed. "You're not an idiot."

Isola wasn't sure he understood what she meant by her bubble. "Globo," she said, "Bubble, not chicle. I get the wrong words. I should've studied Spanish instead of French Renaissance literature."

"You speak fine, but you should practice more."

"True. Did you study any English in México?"

"A little, but I want to take more English classes to get better jobs." He turned away from her.

Isola began to fantasize about all the ways in which she could help Cruz get ahead. Sign him up for classes, get him some job training.

"Tell me more about the Rescate Ángeles. *Who* do they work for?"

"I don't think they work for anybody. They are a small group that struggles against la migra y esos hombres."

"The who?"

"Son rancheros que—"

"The Minutemen." Isola interrupted. Cruz nodded in agreement. "I know about them. I'm not completely clueless, maybe halfway clueless."

"Don't talk that way. Your mother was very proud of you. She said you were muy inteligente."

"Intelligent? She said that?" Isola's words trailed off as she stared at the bright kitchen wallpaper with its oversized lemons and limes.

"Sí." Cruz gave her a look of pity. "It's too bad you didn't come earlier to be with her."

She was at a loss for words and the silence was unbearable. She went to the counter, took a deep breath, and returned with coffee. "How often did you do work for my mother?" Isola filled Cruz's cup.

Cruz helped himself to another bagel. "I came every fifteen days to work in the yard and to help with Rescate or with fixing things around the house."

"Can you tell me about the other Rescate members? I'd like to talk to them."

"They are no longer a group," Cruz said.

"Do you have any of their names or a phone number?"

He shrugged his shoulders. "No, lo siento."

"Shouldn't there should be some information about it in the house?"

"Perhaps. I don't know," he said.

"How long was my mother in Rescate?"

"She was a member until before the cancer. She never told us she was sick. It wasn't good for her to be going to the desert."

"She never told *me* she was sick."

"She didn't tell anybody about her cancer," Cruz said. "I don't know when she started with Rescate."

"When did you cross the border?"

"Three years ago." Cruz answered without hesitation. "I tried crossing five years ago, pero me agarró la migra."

"I guess my mother's work made a difference for you crossing the border."

"Yes. Doña Marina was a strong woman, a martyr."

"That's exactly the word I had in mind. You knew her very well."

"She was a good person. She loved people, was very generous with everybody. She let many people stay at her house."

"I know she was a good person. I *really* do. I should've . . ." She took a deep breath. He reached for her hand and gently squeezed her fingers. He seemed to understand.

"So, you stayed here sometimes?" She pulled her hand away.

"Yes, downstairs. I put the lock in the upstairs room for her. The downstairs was always filled with people who had recently crossed."

"You were her personal handyman?"

"Sí."

"How much did she pay you? I'll give you some money for the—."

Cruz put up his hand. "No, no." He didn't let her finish. "She paid me well. I will help you as a favor to her. She was a good friend too."

"Thank you."

She calculated an appropriate figure. She had to give him something. He hardly knew her and he was going out of his way to help her. She remembered having paid professional movers 600 dollars to haul her bedroom furniture into Gretchen's building. Cruz excused himself to go to the bathroom. Isola waited until he left the room before she slipped him two hundred-dollar bills into the pocket of his denim shirt. She congratulated herself for her quick thinking.

They spent the rest of the day hauling furniture and boxes to Friendly House, Goodwill, and other charitable organizations that her mother had favored. Cruz gave her directions and took the boxes inside while she waited in the comfort of the air-conditioned car. He did all of the heavy, sweaty work for her. The early morning had turned to a violet-streaked evening. Cruz asked to use the shower. She looked for more cash to give. She was grateful for his help and didn't know how to repay him fairly. No one else had been so generous with their time. She didn't care that he had offered not to charge her. She stood to inherit some money and could afford to pay Cruz for his time. She saw how hardworking he was. She wished she had listened to Gretchen and enlisted a friend to help. The cleanup job seemed much easier with another person to talk to, especially when he did most, if not all, of the heavy lifting. Even after their hard work, useless household items and junk littered the garage and house, as if the whole neighborhood had used the residence as its personal dumping ground. The garbage seemed never to end. Her mother had collected outdated calendars from friends and restaurants, school supplies, and old phone books.

"Hasn't she heard about recycling? I'm exhausted."

"You don't have to finish everything today." Cruz walked around and surveyed their progress. He seemed proud of what they had accomplished.

"But I have to clear out the rest before I sell this place."

"I'll come back tomorrow and help you."

Isola thought a moment before answering. "I hate to ask, but I can't do this alone. I can call some movers, I'm sure."

"No, it's no problem. I want to help you. I'll come tomorrow and we can finish. I'll start early. I promise not to disturb your sleep."

"You're too sweet. I promise to make you dinner."

"Deal."

"Deal." Isola laughed at their new game.

7

Liz the Lawyer

The sound of the clock ticking made her aware of how tired she was, but this meeting with the lawyer was important. She could fall asleep in the large armchair if she had a warm blanket. Isola swiveled in the office's armchair, shifting slightly and stopping herself from twirling freely. She kept watch on the door and was startled when she suddenly saw the lawyer watching her from the other side of the room.

"I didn't see you there." She stood and the lawyer greeted her with a warm smile and hug. The hug was a surprise. Liz Martínez had been curt on the phone. She didn't expect Ms. Martínez to be so friendly upon their first in-person meeting.

"My adjoining door is much quieter. I see you've discovered our chairs. Go ahead. Take a full turn. It's fun." Liz Martínez made a twirling motion with her fingers.

"No, sorry. I didn't realize I was fidgeting."

"There's nothing to be sorry about. I do it myself when I'm in my office. Go ahead, take a spin." She seemed determined not to start the meeting until Isola did it. She crossed her arms. Her eyes danced as though calling Isola's bluff.

This must be some sort of test, Isola thought. She felt childish as she obeyed, closed her eyes, and spun in the chair. She made a mental note to let loose more often, something that seemed harder to do as she got older.

"How's the house coming? You're doing a really big job on your own. Are you sure you don't need me to send a cleaning lady or some movers?" Liz pushed a water bottle over to Isola and began sifting through the papers.

"No. I'd rather do it myself. That's why I'm here."

"We have a buyer who's interested. You can go home soon."

"It's complicated," Isola said. "I think I'm going to need more time."

"We can specify a contingency to give you extra time, but I have a buyer who's ready to take the house off your hands. You seemed pretty eager to sell when we last spoke. What's the complication?"

Isola turned to look out the window. The offices looked as though they had been slapped together with no aesthetic architectural concern for the surrounding terrain. Isola thought it a shame not to preserve some of the desert's lonely beauty. She caught herself thinking something her mother would say, "Remember the buffalo" and "how many rooms does one person need?"

Isola recognized a look of controlled impatience on Liz's face. She was having a hard time explaining how the morning's events left her needing more time in the house. The coolness of the air conditioning made it difficult for Isola to think clearly, especially since the temperature outside registered an oppressive 120 degrees.

"A woman and her nephew came to the house. They wanted my father's ID. She said my mother wanted her to have it. I don't know if she was telling the truth, but I can't believe my mother would've sold or given away Dad's identity. She thinks the papers are in the house. That's my complication."

"I've heard worse. That's why I suggested professional movers. You would've had everything shipped to you in San Francisco by now without having to deal with any visitors. Has anyone else been to the house? You only mentioned a woman and her nephew."

"No, that's it. It sounds strange, but they showed up wanting my father's documents. Why all the questions?" Isola had a feeling the lawyer wouldn't approve of Cruz helping her.

"Forgive the third degree. I'm only trying to help you; please remember that. About the woman and her nephew. Marina may have wanted to help them, but you certainly don't have to." The lines on Liz's forehead showed more concern.

"I'm not giving my father's papers to anyone, but maybe there's something else I can do for them. Without involving myself too much." Damn it, there I go again sounding like I can't handle things on my own, she thought.

"It's hard to set boundaries on helping people. Either you help or you don't. Your mother got into some legal trouble for her efforts. Did you know that?"

"Yes," Isola said. "I found her prison release papers in her bedroom. Of course, she never mentioned anything about it. Can you tell me more about the charges?"

"I guess I can break my confidentiality rules this one time."

"I won't tell my mother this one time." They both smiled.

"The neighbors to the east complained of noises in the late hours and called the police. They had some suspicions about the house. Basically they didn't like all the Spanish they heard next door and the different people coming and going. There was a raid or what was supposed to be an investigation and several undocumented people were arrested, along with your mother."

"I'm not surprised. She's been arrested before."

"Phoenix has been very hostile to illegals lately. You can get into a lot of trouble for selling or helping procure false identification cards."

"That's why I need more time. To find my father's documents. They're somewhere in the house."

"If I were you, I'd pack up and leave. You don't want people taking advantage of you. You're young."

"I'm twenty-four."

Liz Martínez gave Isola a smug and satisfied look. "I can see someone easily taking advantage of you. You're about to inherit some money and that amount will double with the sale of your house."

"I better get back to packing." She wanted to get away from the lawyer's critical gaze. She decided not to say anything about Cruz.

"Are you going to sign the paperwork to sell the house?"

"No. Not just yet." Isola walked toward the door. "I'll call you when I'm ready."

When she arrived home, the phone was ringing. Gretchen was the only person who had the house number. Isola left the groceries in the car and ran to pick up the phone.

"Gretchen?" Isola caught her breath. For a second, she thought Cruz might be calling. She remembered giving him her cell, but her mother had probably given him the home number long ago.

"How are you, mija?" Gretchen's voice sounded far away. Isola was relieved it wasn't Cruz calling to cancel on her.

"I'm fine. I've just come from seeing the lawyer." Isola sat at the kitchen table.

"Are you almost done?"

"Far from it." Isola sighed.

"You have some urgent letters. I'm—"

"Did you open the letters?" Isola tried to sound angry, but Gretchen's voice seemed small and fragile.

Silence.

"Yes, that's why I'm calling. There are two urgent ones. Will you be back soon, this week?"

Isola thought about Cruz and Josefina and how she had told Liz Martínez she needed more time in the house. "There's no way I'm getting back this week or next. I have too much to do here. You can't imagine all I have to take care of."

"Marina was my friend. She was the only friend I had when I came from Germany. I've told you the story."

"Yes." Isola sighed. How many times had she heard the story? Her parents loved to tell how they befriended Gretchen and how surprised they were when she had answered them in Spanish when they had thought she only spoke German and a little English. "She eats chiles like candy," her mother once said of her loca friend, la alemana, as she affectionately had called Gretchen.

"Mija, my own mother's been dead for twenty years. Don't you think I can imagine how you feel?"

Isola smiled as she pictured Gretchen's frizzy blonde bob. Gretchen was just like her mother. The two always had to win.

"Just tell me who the letters are from, please," Isola said.

"Mrs. Sánchez."

"That doesn't sound so urgent. Is it life threatening?"

"No."

"Then I'm sure it can wait until I get back. Gretchen, there's no way I can take care of everything at the same time."

"Forget I called."

"I'll see you soon."

"Take care, mija."

"Bye." Isola hung up the phone and decided she'd better start looking into flights to San Francisco. Isola knew there was something else. Gretchen wouldn't bother her over some letters.

8

Doña Trini's Domain

Cruz wandered the streets thinking of a new plan. The foreman at Chandler Rock told him he'd better show his papers if he wanted to work tomorrow. The jefe asked too many questions, but Cruz's bigger problem was where to sleep tonight. The empty house used to be peaceful. He'd almost had a heart attack when doña Marina's daughter discovered him there.

He hoped doña Trini would take him in. If he was lucky, Nacho would be there to convice his aunt to let him stay with them. Without her favorite nephew to soften her up, Trinidad's tongue was more brutal than a Yucatán hurricane. The desert night was warm as usual. Cruz didn't mind walking, but he had to make a decision. He could either go to his favorite cantina or to Trini's house. His chances for shelter would diminish if the old aunt smelled alcohol on him. He crossed the street and waited for the Gilbert bus.

His eyes closed as he sat on the metal bench. The bus's squeal woke him up and he rubbed exhaustion from his eyes before stumbling onto the bus. "Val Vista." He told the driver his stop and settled for a seat at the back of the bus.

The cars passing by blurred until Cruz closed his eyes. The bus came to an abrupt halt. Cruz's body rocked from side to side, waking him. "Val Vista, Val Vista," the driver shouted.

Cruz crossed the street and could see Trini's lit porch from two blocks away. The ranch-style house seemed quiet, but the neighborhood wasn't. He heard music from a backyard; a woman's cinnamon-stick voice sang romantic ballads. Cruz checked his pockets. He had forgotten to bring a gift or some flowers. Trini would become your best friend if you brought her a trash-rescued piece of jewelry. In one of his sleepless strolls, the moon shone on a heart-shaped pendant missing its clasp and chain. He picked it up, buffed it. Nacho had taught Cruz how easy it was to win his aunt's affections. He was right and he couldn't go there empty-handed. He checked his wallet. He carried a few dollars and change, but not enough money for a bribe. There was no way he was going to give up the two crisp hundreds Isola had put in his wallet. He had other plans for the money and they didn't include Trinidad.

Cruz opened the side gate and walked toward Trini's backyard. He saw two men at a card table, relaxing, drinking beer with their feet propped up on each side of the wobbly table.

"¿Se encuentra Trini?"

The men looked up at each other, but not at him. Cruz wondered if they heard him. He didn't wait for an answer.

He had heard Trini boast enough times about how the house belonged to her and no one else. He unlatched the gate, stepped inside, and then heard barking. He was halfway between the gate and the backdoor that led to Trini's laundry room when he heard a noise like rolling thunder and a woman crying. Cruz turned to the two men sitting back, finishing off their last beer. The heavier guy stood up and raised his hand. But it didn't help Cruz's fall. In two seconds, he was on his back with a fist-sized paw on his chest and a wet tongue lapping his nose and tugging on his ears. He closed his eyes and shielded his face until someone pulled the dog off him. The other guy with the long Zapata mustache jeered and enjoyed the show. Cruz left the two men laughing with their dog. He dusted himself off in the laundry room and caught his breath. He could still hear them cackling and praising the puppy for being "a good little watchdog."

Trini's bedroom was down the hall to the left of the kitchen's refrigerator. The lights were off in the kitchen except for a dim lamp over the stove. Cruz took one deep breath and opened the kitchen door. Upon reaching the hallway, he heard a door opening and the creaking of heavy footsteps.

Trini opened her arms and enveloped Cruz in her girth. She allowed Cruz to step back and come up for air.

"What did you bring me this time, mijo? Another heart? A necklace for my pendant?"

"No, señora Trinidad." Cruz bowed his head and shuffled his feet. Why hadn't he brought something? He should have buffed one of those rocks from the quarry supply, looked through more dumpsters along the way, something. "Who are those guys out there and when did you get that dog?"

"The dog belongs to my nephews from San Carlos. The boys plan on fighting him; he won't hurt you. King's a puppy. Eloy and Manuel got them at the swap meet yesterday." Trini walked toward the kitchen and took a seat.

"There's more?"

"Only two, the puppy and Chacho—he's in a cage. Did you come in from the side? You should've knocked at the front."

"I didn't want to disturb your novela, doña Trini. I just wanted to ask if you can spare a room for me tonight?" He sat down.

"A room?" Trini gurgled and coughed dramatically. She could be a drama queen when she wanted to. "I'm the only one who gets a room in my house. Who do you think pays the bills around here?"

"I mean a place to sleep for tonight."

"How much money do you have?"

"Tres dólares." Cruz emptied out his pockets. "But I can pay more next week."

"Three dollars? Why don't you get a job like mija? Pifi makes good money and the boss lady gives her a room of her own. My niece is an angel. Pifi slips me an extra bill when she makes good tips from the rich people who can afford to hire mija to clean their houses. God rest her mother's soul."

"I'm working on getting a job, Trini." Cruz made the sign of the cross in reverence of the memory of Pifi's mother.

Trini looked up at the stove's clock. "I can't believe you're asking me for a favor five minutes before my novela starts. I need to know what happens to Lucero when she finds out her chulo's making love to his cousin, that evil Felipa. You'll have to wait." Trini's words trailed off as she walked down the hallway and rattled her keys before closing her bedroom door behind her. Cruz wasn't sure if he could stay. He heard every overacted scene. It was during a Crisco commercial that Cruz heard Trini stir. Her heavy body caused her unsteady bed to creak and chirp.

Trini slowly walked toward Cruz. She stood before him for several seconds before showing signs of pity.

45

"For you, mi flaco, you can sleep on the kitchen table for your three dollars. But you'll have to shower first and sleep in the nude. God only knows where those filthy clothes have been. I'm not a hotel. You'll have to pay me later for the wash and shower." Trini smiled and showed her old fillings and the rotten tooth that smelled, oddly, of old bubblegum.

Cruz had heard about Trini's distasteful sense of humor. She could've said no when he walked in the door. But the vieja took pleasure in feeling important. Cruz wanted to laugh at her joke, but was too tired to indulge the old tía.

"You can stay today, but I don't want to see your face tomorrow night." Trini laid a chubby fist on the table. She left Cruz standing in the kitchen. She didn't have a scrap of rug to spare. "Tenga." Trini shuffled back with a pillow and a torn-up blanket in her arms.

"Don't worry about the dogs. They won't come into my house."

Cruz was worried, but not about the dogs. He tried to drown out the Spanish news from the television set in Trini's bedroom by humming to himself. He chose a corner in the carpeted dining room, where Trini's other relatives snored on the couches.

9

Dusty Photographs

Isola squinted at the sliver of sunlight prying open her eyes. Her mouth tasted sour and her neck was sore from falling asleep on the couch. She rinsed her mouth in the faucet and took in the kitchen's puke-green walls for the first time. What were you thinking, Mother? Lemons and limes? You never liked green.

Isola was OK with the lemony-bright yellow curtains, but not the lime. The lime was more of a faint guacamole or *Exorcist* thick pea-soup color. She looked up. The clock read 6:30. She found her cup of coffee on the bistro table where Cruz had sat only hours ago. While she waited for the microwave to heat her cup, she opened the bottom drawer, the very last cabinet, the one she hadn't opened while searching for the coffee.

"Jackpot," she said.

In some ways, her mother had never changed. She remembered the dinosaur drawer, as she had called it, from her days before the big blow-up. Her mother had a habit of keeping old photographs, especially ones she didn't like of herself, in the kitchen's bottom drawer, farthest away from the refrigerator. Isola didn't remember when her mother had started the tradition.

However, instead of finding unflattering photos of her mother, Isola discovered a treasure trove of her childhood. Underneath a package of microcassettes for her mother's answering machine was a photograph of herself as a skinny little girl. Her green eyes matched her green dress. She remembered how she used to strain her ankles to form a straight line with her shiny black Mary Janes and splay her feet 180 degrees like Mary Poppins.

More picture frames. Isola riding a caramel pony in Golden Gate Park; Isola standing in a strawberry field with other small children, the date stamp read 03-23-75; and a black-and-white photo of herself playing dress-up with her mother's fur coat. Her father had spent a small fortune on the beaver coat, only for her mother to burn it in protest. Her father loved to tell the story about how covering the Farm Workers Union and meeting César Chávez had altered their upward mobility in society forever. He and his wife had become devoted to Chávez's cause. Isola remembered never eating grapes and protesting with her parents her entire childhood, but she had become completely disillusioned by her mother's activism in San Francisco and constant protesting and campaigning for Jerry Brown, a man whose political career never ended. The campaigning meant Isola had never gotten to do what she wanted. She was especially unhappy about the fact that her father had always been away, covering the lives of other people, other families, and other children for the *San Francisco Chronicle*.

The last photo in the drawer was of her and Jeremy at the Berkeley Marina. The picture belonged in the dinosaur drawer. Isola was surprised her mother had held onto the photograph for all these years. On the other hand, her mother had never accepted her break-up with Jeremy. She always seemed to enjoy opposing her, especially when it came to her love life. Dwelling on these photos by herself was not a good idea. She felt the inertia sink in. She shoved everything in a box and labeled it "Dinosaur Drawer" and rushed to the grocery store.

10

Dinner Guest

Isola opened the door to a bedraggled Cruz. Why hadn't she prepared a more substantial meal for him? He was her guest, she reminded herself. She wished she knew how to cook the kind of feast her mother used to prepare, a dizzying assortment of homemade tortillas, rice, salsa, beef in a thick soupy sauce, and a generous bowl of guacamole. No matter how expensive the avocados were, her mother always served thick chunks of avocado with cilantro and lime, her father's favorite.

Isola was in her mother's sundress again. Should she change? It's not a date, she reminded herself. More important, had she bought the sausages, along with all of the deli foods? Isola worried about her sanity. How was she going to get back to her publications and studies when she couldn't even remember what she bought at the supermarket earlier that day? Seeing Cruz again seemed to make all those worries far away and unimportant. She reminded herself she was on a well-deserved leave of absence.

"Have you been working all this time?" Isola ushered Cruz out of the evening heat and led him into the kitchen.

Cruz eyed her, studied her as though he were trying to decide if he could trust her. "Working is easier," he said, "than asking doña Trini for a place to live."

He said more things in Spanish about doña Trini than Isola understood. She had trouble understanding the closed-mouth Spanish of México, a speech much faster than California Spanish.

"I thought we settled this already. I told you to stay here," Isola said. "¿Quién es doña Trini?"

While he spoke, Isola dreamed up all sorts of plans to help Cruz with the services he needed, maybe get him into an apartment so he wouldn't have to ask other people for places to stay. She was just as resourceful as her mother and could help out one person. However, she was too embarrassed to tell him about her fantasy plans for him. She didn't want to scare him off. She saw, in the unsure way he sat at the small dining table, that he had much pride.

"Doña Trinidad is the aunt of my friend Nacho."

Isola almost sat down to hear the story, but started to pull out food from the refrigerator instead.

"I found a good grocery store with lots of my favorite foods. I hope you like them too."

"You are so generous. I am sure I will love everything." He said the word "love" as he gazed directly into her eyes.

She dismissed his compliment and looked away as she unwrapped cheeses, breads, jalapeño-stuffed olives, mango salsa, sushi rolls, hummus, grape leaves, salami, and bean dip.

Cruz's eyes widened. He stared at the food as though he had been served live worms.

She feared the array was too exotic for him. She should've gotten take-out from El Pollo Grande. Maybe the sausages would make up for the international goulash.

"Ándale, come," she said. "Get started while I cook the sausages." She handed him a plate and scooped hummus on a blue corn chip and fed it to him. She was happy when he helped himself to more.

"Trini was a good friend of my mother's. She used to treat me like family, but now she has her own nephews to take care of. Nacho puts in a good word for me, but he's not always around. I'm waiting for a space at Thornton or Alberto's."

"Are those housing units?"

"No. Jobs that have housing for workers."

"Do they have your phone number?"

"No. I didn't take a chance on giving them Trini's number. I check with them every now and then. Sometimes they have work for me to do."

"Why can't you trust Trini with the number?"

"I cannot trust her with anything. I used to give her the bulk of my paychecks and she'd only offer a corner of her floor in the front room. She gave the cot that I left at her house to her nephew Óscar. If she hears about the job, she will tell one of them to go instead of giving me my message."

"Why did you have a falling out?"

"We didn't," Cruz said, "that's the funny thing." He opened the grape leaf with the stuffed rice and olives and smelled it before he popped it into his mouth. "When people tell you you're family and they are not your blood relatives, they'll stab you harder in the heart." Cruz scooped up more of the sand-colored mash on a tortilla chip.

"You're a poet, Cruz Zárate!" She nudged his arm.

"No, that's one of abuelita's dichos."

"That may be one of your grandmother's sayings, but you weren't thinking about your grandmother or doña Trini. Am I right?"

Cruz shook his head. "Qué inteligente eres."

"Stop with the 'inteligente' business. Anyone can see you have a faraway look in your eyes. So who's the girl?"

"I was thinking about Rosalina, my brother's wife."

"Calling someone intelligent sounds like a bad joke. Sometimes Gretchen calls me that when she's being annoying and sarcastic. Anyone can tell you were in love with your brother's wife."

Cruz blushed.

"You don't have to say anything more." Isola turned off the stove.

"It was a long time ago," he said, "and she is my brother's wife."

"The onions are a little crisp, but they're good that way." She scooped the greasy mound out of the pan.

Cruz seemed to perk up at the sight of the big platter of greasy meat and onions Isola plopped in front of him.

"Todo está muy sabroso," Cruz said. He rubbed his belly like a child.

Isola enjoyed his silliness. Sharing a simple meal with Cruz, a stranger, was so much easier than the last meal she had had with Jeremy before their breakup, the one filled with the silence that said they'd never again be able to do something as natural as share a meal together.

"Trini must live far from here?"

51

"No. Her house is here in Chandler. It is easy to find. On Ray Road, before Chandler Boulevard, there is a small street also called Chandler and her house is at the end of the road. The yellow house with plastic white ducks in the front yard and jasmine flowers covering the front door. The same white flowers in front of your house." Cruz flapped his arms in a circle to show the ducks were lawn windmills.

Isola laughed a warm pink laugh at his flapping duck imitation.

"How long have you had the problem with Trini?"

"I thought I would always have a place at her house. I had my own bed, a cot your mother had given me in exchange for cleaning the swimming pool. But her mijo came and bought these mean dogs." He opened his eyes wide as though his entire face held back a sneeze. Finally, a tear escaped. He quickly flicked the fat drop away, as though fanning a fly from his nose. She pretended not to notice.

"That's it. You're staying here. End of discussion." She waited until she sensed that Cruz and she had an agreement. The deal was sealed with a handshake. Cruz laughed and shook his head.

"I'm serious."

"I know you're serious. You are too generous. Next time, you let me cook for you."

"You know how to cook?"

"Sí, carne asada." Cruz tapped his chest.

Isola laughed at the high volume of his voice. He must be really proud of his grilling, she thought.

"All men know how to use a grill," she said. "It's a deal."

They shook hands again. Outside crickets chirped loudly and the cicadas hissed like the sound of maracas.

"Cuéntame de tu vida en San Francisco."

"Oh, it's a long, boring story. Nothing exciting. I'll tell you another time. I promise." She started walking around the house looking for her wallet, her phone. "I need to go to San Francisco tomorrow and get some more of my things."

Cruz sat down; his eyes followed her. He started to say something, but closed his mouth. He looked at her with pity, as though she were a bird with broken wings about to be pounced on by cat. He started to stand, but she held out her hand and motioned for him to stay. He obeyed.

"I'm sorry I need to do this now. I thought I'd only be staying here a few days or a week, but I have too much to do here. You eat. I'll get you some towels and a blanket. You can sleep on the couch." Isola left Cruz seated at the table and checked on him as she made her arrangements. She called for flights and a cab ride to the airport. "Everything will be better when I get back," she said. "Don't worry. I know I seem crazy, but now that you're staying here, I don't have to worry about the house being empty or my stuff."

Cruz listened to her make plans. "Can I help?"

"No, thanks." She felt his eyes on her as she darted around the house. "Sit down, I'll be right back."

When she came back down from packing her suitcase, he had washed the dishes and put them away. She rested towels and a blanket on the couch.

"You are going on the plane now?" Cruz emphasized each word.

"Yes. I found a flight. And it leaves in two hours. I think these will work." She checked the extra keys on the front door and handed them to Cruz.

"¿Pero qué te pasa?" Cruz still seemed bewildered. He put the keys in his back pocket.

"I'm always like this." She lied. Even she wasn't used to her own whims. "Can you ignore my crazy impulses? Are we still friends? You're going to stay here, right?"

Cruz laughed. "Yes," he said, "don't worry about me."

"I'm sorry to leave so quickly. We had a nice meal. Yes?"

"Yes," he said in English.

"Good."

"Good," he repeated.

She heard a loud car honk. "Eat the rest of the food, OK?"

He shrugged his shoulders and made a sad face like a clown.

She laughed at his goofy frown.

"How did you manage to arrange everything so quickly?"

"A trick I learned from my mother. The flight's expensive, but oh, well. Thanks again. I appreciate you understanding me."

They shook hands once again.

11

Back to La Barda

Cruz arrived at la barda too late. His usual spot in front of the Mesa gas station was crowded with men he had never seen before. Friday was never a good day for finding work. The foreman hired new crews on Monday and most of the jobs lasted through the week, usually until Friday and sometimes Saturday. Men crowded into the few trucks that crawled by. Today Cruz didn't have ganas and wasn't as eager or as hungry as the rest of the men.

He'd rather spend more time with Isola and help her. Working for her was like being in a dream he never wanted to wake up from. He thought about how strange it was to meet Isola and how stupid he had been for going to the house and getting caught. Now that he had met her, he didn't want to leave her. How he wanted to take her offer, live with her and not worry about working like a dog. He could easily do it, but it was wrong. He had promised Marina that he would never look at her daughter. She had often obsessed about the fact that her daughter was younger and prettier and that he would find her attractive and fall in love with her. How quickly he had broken his promise to Marina. Marina was right. He had found her daughter irresistible. He started fantasizing about Isola. If he married her, he'd get his citizenship, have a nice house to live in, a young, beautiful wife who would have lots of babies. He'd be a king in America. Don't be stupid, he thought, something will crush you and your plan like a boot stomping a cucaracha. He had lost the two women he had fallen in love with, first Rosalina and now Marina. It was his strange fate.

Isola was different, he told himself. Then he faced reality. She'd never fall for him. She was a lonely girl whose mother had died. He had lived long enough to know how grief affects the heart. Her feelings for him wouldn't last. And he liked her too much to take advantage of her. She was a sweet girl. Confused and crazy, but sweet. He had to forget—really forget—about staying with her. He'd work for his keep and beg Trini for a place to stay, and not bother doña Marina's daughter!

In his reverie, he didn't notice the man standing behind him until he felt a firm hand on his shoulder. He had almost forgotten he was still at la barda, waiting for work.

"Oye, hermano. You got to climb in the truck. Let the driver kick you out if he doesn't need you."

Cruz stepped away to release himself from the man's grasp. He turned to see who was calling him "brother." The older man wasn't even a cousin, but his sagging cheeks and the way they flapped when he talked reminded Cruz of his mother's older brother, Amado.

"¿Y tú, tío? Did you miss the last car to tell me that?"

"No. I came for the cheap burritos and to watch pendejos like you."

Cruz walked away from the bent-over man who was too old to find work. If the man weren't so well dressed, Cruz might've taken him for a payaso, a clown who insults men for a handout, just like his poor tío Amado.

"Wait. I can get you a job. But it's at night," the man said.

"At night, doing what?"

"Cutting the phone books. Go to Bell phone company by Papago Park. Tell them Elorio sent you."

"Tell who?"

"Miguel Murillo, the foreman."

"Gracias," Cruz said. Ideas coursed through his mind. He liked the idea of not hammering gravel in the hot sun and sleeping during the day.

"De nada."

"¿Y la mordida?"

"The foreman's my nephew. He cuts me some reales when I bring him workers, gives me a little extra if a man has papers. He'll treat you real good if you mention me."

Cruz had never thought about working at night. But he was willing to try anything. Doña Trini might give him a place to sleep during the day. A car with a choked muffler approached. A stream of PMEX gas fumes filled Cruz's nostrils. The truck rolled by slowly. The driver had a passenger, but didn't pick up anybody. Nacho had warned him not to get in cars that had come from the border. He had heard too many stories about the coyotes selling out their cargo to la migra, the ranchers, or drug traffickers as slave labor. He wasn't about to take any chances.

The next truck picked up four men. Cruz officially ended his job search for the day. He had no choice but to approach Trini again. The house wasn't going to stay empty forever and Isola had plans to sell it when she returned. This time he'd ask for a place to sleep during the day instead of at night. He convinced himself it was a good plan for everyone. He was confident Trini would agree. Hadn't he given her the bulk of his first paychecks? Hadn't he bought her furniture and helped her around the house?

He took the East Valley Bus to Chandler Boulevard and walked the three long blocks to doña Trini's. Her street was busy. Cruz had to think if he wasn't off by a day. Was it Friday or Saturday already? He heard music as he approached Trini's house, but it wasn't coming from her television. It was a recording of Cuco Sánchez belting out one of his sad songs. He opened the back gate even though the señora always bugged him about his not knocking on her front door. She enjoyed being difficult sometimes. Trini always kept the front door locked and never opened it on account of the "alelullias," as she called the people who peddled God and Bibles and always asked for money. He was halfway to the back door when he heard a succession of deep low growls coming from behind him. Cruz screamed and flew out the front gate. He had turned around and run so fast that he didn't see what kind of dog or wolf chased him. In all the years he had known Trinidad López, both in Arizona and Atlixco, Cruz had never known her to keep vicious dogs.

Trini flung open the door, allowing the screen to slam them in.

"I thought that was you. What's going on?"

"Ay! I thought it was another dog."

"No seas dramático. Chato bought King at a discount. You've seen him before."

"Son malos los pit bulls. Be careful with that animal."

"King only harms escuincles such as yourself. The other day he was being so cute." Trini stopped talking and looked at the clock. "Se me va el tiempo. What do you want? Nacho and them are working. Why aren't you working? Don't tell me you want money!"

"No, señora."

"Pues, my novela's going to start before I finish el quehacer."

"How should I say it?" Cruz knew he shouldn't ask anything of Trini before her novela. He had forgotten in the excitement of his new plan.

"Spit it out! I have to finish the rice and meat before I hear the pleito about Lupe's sister's husband."

"I was thinking I could sleep here during the day and work at night."

Trini stood silent. An eerie smile bloomed across her face like a sunflower past its prime. Her eyes twinkled and she seemed unusually happy, as though she'd dance a malagueña.

"¿Entonces?" Cruz didn't want to be impatient, but he had to change the strange expression on Trini's mouth.

He jumped back at Trini's explosive laughter. She grabbed the top layer of her overflowing belly and spat wet laughter through her missing tooth.

"Sleep during the day to work at night." She twirled like a circus elephant. She held onto the door frame to catch her breath. "Hijo, you know how to give a vieja a good laugh. Why can't you be as inventive with getting a better job?"

"But I am being inventive."

"Do you expect me to turn over my house to you because you're a clever young man with crazy ideas? ¡No, hombre, ni lo mande Dios!"

Trini crossed herself, laughed some more, and took several breaths before padding down the hallway to her bedroom to pour herself a cup of her Sparkletts water. Cruz heard the loud gurgle of Trini's personal water dispenser. She never offered the expensive Sparkletts water to anyone else. She emerged in the kitchen refreshed and holding the empty paper cone. Her smile and laughter deflated as she checked on her food. An even bigger change transformed her. She moved as though Cruz were not in the room, as though he had never stopped by to see her. Cruz almost didn't recognize her face.

Trini lifted the top of the big olla on the stove and released a warm swirl of smoke and a whiff of beans, onion, and cilantro.

He sat at the kitchen table, facing away from Trini. He was too dejected to move. Cruz could tell the beans were ready, but he didn't dare ask Trini for a small bowl.

She strained jalapeños, onions, tomatoes, and garlic and then ground them in a blender. His mother had only used a molcajete. She preferred how the chiles tasted against the stone mortar. He knew Trini had cut the meat and would cook the rice last. His mouth watered, and he didn't care that he'd be having an Americanized version of doña Trini's meal at the Taco Bell or Alberto's Taquería.

Trini worked quietly.

Her silence was stronger than any of her previous refusals. Cruz left as Trini started to cut the meat into cubes and prepare a hot meal for her nephews. Funny, he had always thought of her as family.

Cruz knew he had asked for too much. He stood and walked out without looking back. The screen door slammed and its echo trilled hollow in his ear. He had no choice but to stay another night at doña Marina's house.

12

Epifanía

Epifanía finished scrubbing the toilet and bathtub in Adele's bedroom. She threw the white cotton underwear in the laundry basket. She thought la dama had no shame because she never picked up after herself. Adele was the only client she wanted to drop from her list, an impossible dream since Adele was her employer. Epifanía thought Adele was more like a child than an old widow. There was nothing to be done about her habits. Epifanía couldn't fire her boss, the woman who gave her a free room and kept food in the refrigerator that she was always "welcomed to." The señora pretended to be so sophisticated and Epifanía didn't understand why Adele had trouble putting her chones in the hamper. Instead, Adele left her underwear wherever she took it off, by her dresser, on the counter, near the shower. Epifanía sometimes found the loose things while making the bed.

Having to touch people's underwear was part of the reason why Epifanía always kept her gloves on until she was sure her work was completed. She was disgusted by Adele's habits, but she kept reminding herself of all the benefits the job offered. Paid groceries, nice hand-me-downs, and more important, her boss let her borrow her passport and wigs when she needed to visit her mother in Atlixco. Adele's wig, along with a thick slather of makeup, made Epifanía look older. She was proud of the few times she had crossed the border without getting caught. Epifanía didn't know of any other boss who was so generous. She didn't care that her brother Nacho thought the old lady took advantage of her. At least she didn't have to sleep in a crowded apartment with people she didn't know.

Epifanía turned on the fan. She heard the screen door crash shut and went to see what that was all about. Adele was hidden behind several shopping bags cutting into her arms. She walked in sniffing the air with a twisted face, as though she smelled something dead.

"I told you not to use those harsh chemicals in my house. Use those for our other clients, not in the house. Don't you understand I bought the organic products for here?" Adele threw down all her bags and wiped her forehead with a dramatic sweep of her white handkerchief as though the act of eliminating a few drops of sweat would make the world more tolerable.

"Sí, señora Adele. I'm sorry." Epifanía rushed to help with her bags.

Epifanía knew that "organic products" meant overpriced cleaners that didn't work as well as the name brands her tía Trini used. Her Ajax, Tide, Clorox, and Pine-Sol kept her from having to strain her arms with scrubbing so hard or from using her nails to get to crevices the organic products didn't clean.

"You're back early."

"We have a crisis! That's why my shopping was interrupted." Adele sat on her favorite love seat, propped up her feet, and sighed.

"¿Qué paso?" Epifanía restrained herself from rushing to wipe off the clay dirt from Adele's sandals.

"I need you to take on another client for this week until I replace Candie."

"Who's Candie?" Epifanía tightened a curl and tucked the roller under her scarf.

"Candelaria Pilar Guzmán Gutiérrez. She wanted to be called Candie. She quit Mr. Schmidt's home. It's up to you to fill in."

"But I don't have time for another one. How about Vero?" Epifanía took off her apron and brought Adele a diet Coke with lots of ice and a straw.

Adele nodded and mumbled a thank you.

Epifanía barely heard what she said. She sat quietly. She knew Adele had more to say.

"I see you have your hair in rollers. Is that why you don't want to go?" Adele adjusted her orange wig, the one that made her look like Lucille Ball's mother.

"No, I'm not going out tonight. It's that I have more than enough clients for this week."

"Are you trying to say I'm working you too hard?"

"Sí, señora. I mean, no."

"That's not what I heard. Verónica says you don't want any new clients you can't train." Adele leaned back in the blue upholstered armchair and smiled as though she were keeping a big secret. She rested her feet on the matching ottoman and flexed her toes.

"I don't know what she means," Epifanía said.

"You only want customers who leave a clean house for you." Adele slipped her feet back in her sandals and stood tall.

"I always do my work."

"I'm not denying that. I'm saying that when Verónica filled in for you she was surprised to hear the clients apologizing for leaving specs of dust behind the door."

"Verónica es una exagerada."

"You don't have to apologize."

"Pero, I never . . ."

"Listen. I know you're wildly popular. I don't understand how you get away with it and I don't care as long you do the work I ask you to. Do I need to say more?" She took a single step toward Epifanía, held high the piece of paper with the client's address in black marker and set it down by the lamp.

"No, señora." Epifanía used her loud, commanding voice to answer. She quickly turned around and read the paper, then wadded it into her pocket. Epifanía didn't want to go to a new client's house to clean, even if Mr. Schmidt's address was close by, only four blocks away.

"Finish up here. Don't take more than fifteen minutes. Take the company car, but I want to see the car back in the driveway in two hours." Adele went into her bedroom and locked the door.

Epifanía wondered if she could get away with keeping the company car so she wouldn't be late meeting Cruz and Nacho. She'd better not take any chances under the old lady's watchful eye. I'll work fast, even if it's not the best job I do, she thought, but what if this man's a real cochino?

"Are you listening to me?" Adele called through the door.

"Sí, señora," she yelled. Epifanía turned to put her kit away and get fresh gloves for the new client's house; she wasn't sure what she'd find over there. She took off her yellow gloves and gave a salute to Adele's closed bedroom door.

As if she saw through the walls, Adele unlocked the door, stuck her head out, and stared at Epifanía. She had taken off her wig and false eyelashes and looked like a clown. Epifanía pinched the skin above her elbow to keep from laughing.

"¿Señora?"

"That box needs to go in the fridge." Adele closed her door. "You can help yourself to those ribs and anything else left in there." She yelled from her bedroom. "After you finish at Mr. Schmidt's."

Epifanía stuck out her tongue. She wasn't hungry for leftover ribs.

13

Frisco Fog

Isola's cab arrived. The evening sky bloomed in broad bands of orange, yellow, and magenta, wild colors to match her scattered mood. The overpriced ticket was a necessary expense. She had been mistaken in thinking Marina had spent her entire inheritance and she was genuinely surprised that her mother hadn't left any money to her relatives in México. Then again, it was befitting of her mother to leave her only daughter the choice to be charitable on her own accord.

"That will be twenty-five dollars, Miss."

"Excuse me?" It seemed as though only minutes had passed since she had closed her eyes. The cab driver was already at her airline terminal.

"Twenty-five dollars." The man, Indian, she guessed, pointed to the meter.

She cleared security and was quickly seated. She hadn't realized how close she had been to missing her plane. The flight seemed as swift as the cab ride to the airport. If it weren't for the half-dozen cell phone messages from the lawyer's office in Tempe, she might have assumed her Phoenix stay and meeting Cruz had been one of those dreams you couldn't explain. The faint twinkling lights from south San Francisco below reminded her of why she was running back and forth like a mad woman. She needed to get things rolling, understand her mother's life before selling the house, and help Cruz, her one selfless act.

She asked the concierge at baggage claim for help hailing a cab. She usually took BART into town, but didn't think the buses and trains were running so late, nor was she willing to freeze to death by researching her options. She felt nude, cold and exposed in her Capri pants and pink cotton twinset. She sucked in the evening air. How quickly her body had adapted to the desert nights. The cab driver, a woman, offered her a blanket. Was she dreaming? Cab drivers had never been so nice to her before. Isola draped the thick wool over her lap. She thought of her feather bed and down comforter in her apartment. Sleep in her own bed was a welcomed thought. She bumped her elbow on the window as the cab exited Army Street and hit the pothole Isola was always quick to avoid.

"Are you warm enough back there?" The cab driver had an East Coast accent. Vowels lingered on her tongue like sticky peanut butter.

"Yes, thank you," Isola said.

Even without the accent, the way the driver turned the yellow cab and raced up the hills made Isola think she wasn't a local. A New Yorker, no doubt. She was glad the woman got her to her apartment in one piece. Isola felt too exhausted to get lost or give directions. She was grateful the driver wasn't too chatty. Again, she thought only of sleep and her warm bed.

It was almost midnight. Isola rushed to get out of the cold air. She tried not to make any noise, but then again, maybe she should make her presence known. It suddenly dawned on her that she hadn't given Gretchen any warning that she was coming back today. Isola thought it best not to disturb the other tenants. She tiptoed to the top floor, key ready in hand, treading as softly as possible, but noticed there was noise coming from her apartment. A light shone from the half-inch space underneath the door. Isola remembered congratulating herself for convincing Gretchen to pull up the carpeting in her apartment and polish the hardwood floors. However, allowing Gretchen to do her a favor had its price, like the way she often let herself into the apartment. Gretchen had probably gotten something from the kitchen and left the light on. The old woman took such liberties. Isola heard more noises. The light wasn't as bothersome as the voices she heard coming from inside her apartment. She was tired, but lucid enough to discern talking and heavy breathing in the bedroom. She placed her bag on the floor and put her hand on the knob. It didn't appear to be locked, the way she had left it.

Isola opened the door. Her skin felt clammy. She took a deep breath and remembered how useless her fear had been when it was Cruz she had discovered in her mother's house. However, it was impossible not to fear the squeaking of bed springs and the loud moaning as she approached her bedroom. Jeremy still had a key. If it was Jeremy acting out some sick fantasy, she was going to lose it. And she'd make sure he'd lose something as well.

She snapped on more lights and made noise as she released her bags with a crashing thud on the hardwood floors. She was no longer afraid as she heard a rustling of blankets and covers, then recognized her sheets and comforter billowing before her. Blank faces stared back at her. She didn't recognize the couple. The man certainly was not Jeremy. The guy in her bed was much older, with a beach-ball belly. The blonde woman was attractive and much younger than the man.

The woman cussed in German. Isola recognized the woman yelling the word *dummkopf* and Gretchen's name. Of course Gretchen had to be behind this mess. The naked coupled continued to argue.

"Aren't you going to say anything to me? You're in my bed. Get out!" Isola circled them.

They had lit the candle her mother had given her. Never mind that they had left a glass of wine on her original edition of *Queen Margot's Memoir*, and an ashtray on top of her collection of sixteenth-century books. But she couldn't forgive them for using the white candle shaped like a baby seal. Her mother had bought it in Carmel and Isola had wanted to preserve that souvenir forever and never burn it. These people had used it to enhance their lovemaking ambiance. She wanted to slap them.

One of her pewter knights had fallen off the bookshelf. She picked it up and placed the knight in her pocket instead of returning the figurine next to the four miniatures from her visit to Westminster Abbey during her first summer in college.

The couple continued to argue while Isola surveyed the rest of the damage to her belongings.

"Go argue somewhere else. You're in *my* bed." Isola raised her voice and was startled when they began yelling at her.

All three of them jumped at the banging of the wall. Apparently, the booming bang was Gina in the apartment downstairs, her usual solution for demanding some sleep and quiet.

At last, she heard the clump of Gretchen's familiar footsteps on the stairs.

As she entered the apartment, Gretchen tied the sash around her worn pink robe and smoothed back her short gray curls. "Keep your voices down!" "Keep my voice down? There's naked people in my bed." Isola pointed at the couple.

"I didn't know you were coming home today." Gretchen spat out the words. "What do you mean you didn't know! Does it matter? I still live here as far as I know. I don't want random people using my apartment. This isn't *my* fault. Weren't *you* the one who called *me* with a message about some *urgent* letters?" She didn't notice she was screaming at the top of her voice until Gretchen lightly touched her shoulder.

"Ya, ya, mein intelligentes Mädchen," Gretchen said. She rattled off another stream of words. Too quick for Isola to understand with her rusty high-school German. "I understand you're upset. I thought you were supposed to stay in Arizona to settle your mother's estate. You're back early, even though the letters, as you say, are not *life threatening* to mademoiselle." She continued to talk down to Isola. Gretchen's voice smacked of sarcasm as she recalled their earlier conversation. Isola remembered how her mother used to do the same thing to her.

Isola didn't care that she was making a spectacle of herself or that she was disturbing Gina's sleep. She wanted to disturb everyone's sleep. She had paid her rent and Gretchen had gone too far this time with the liberties she took as the landlady and her mother's friend. "Do you lease out everyone's apartment while they're away on business or vacation?" She spoke slowly. She wanted Gretchen to fix the situation right away.

"Hush. Listen. My brother and his new wife are here from Germany. I should've told you and—"

"You should've *asked* me. God, Gretchen."

"I was going to tell you that I needed your apartment when you got back."

"But it's my apartment. I pay rent, even when I don't pay my student loans or my credit cards. You can't just use it whenever you want to."

"It's for my brother. I've been giving you a good deal on the room because of your mother. Now you have that house and money. You can get another place. My brother and Adelheid are moving here."

The woman slipped on a shirt and retreated to the bathroom. Gretchen's brother stood up and followed her. He didn't bother covering his naked ass.

"A good deal? You've known me all my life. You've only seen your 'brother' once or twice in Germany." Isola couldn't contain herself. She wanted to scream her lungs out across the bay, summon the help of someone, anyone.

"Isola, you're tired. You need some sleep. We will sort things out in the morning."

"And where am I going to sleep? Do you know what they were doing in my bed?"

"Enough, mija. I'll make up the cot for you."

"Oh, now it's 'mija.' I don't want a cot. I want my bed. That's my bed." She paused a moment and felt she could almost read Gretchen's mind: Technically, the four-poster bed crammed into the bedroom was hers and not Isola's. What difference did it make, Isola thought; it was still her bed, her apartment.

"Come upstairs for one minute. I'll change the sheets for you and you can sleep in your bed. I'll give them mine and I'll take the cot. We'll talk tomorrow."

Isola noted the switch from smarmy sarcasm to the businesslike lilt in Gretchen's voice. Gretchen no longer spoke to Isola as though she were her family. Isola had once spent a whole summer at Gretchen's while her parents were in Europe. She wasn't used to her business-only voice, the one she used for her other tenants. Gretchen's tone made Isola remember Cruz's words about Trini and blood ties: *When people tell you you're family and they are not your blood relatives, they'll stab you harder in the heart.*

14

Mommy Marina

San Francisco, 1983

Marina carried the typewriter over to the kitchen table. She plugged the cord into the socket and began typing fast, clicking strokes that sounded as if she were dancing flamenco. Usually Isola enjoyed listening to her mother use the typewriter and reading the letter over her shoulder. However, now she sulked in the hallway and pulled at her Strawberry Shortcake pajamas. She knew all about the letter her mother was writing and she didn't like it one bit. She couldn't complain to her father because he had called from his desk to say he was going to be late again. Her mother had explained to her several times that they weren't giving her away to Gretchen, that she and her father only wanted to make sure Gretchen would have the "proper authority" to take her to the hospital or to pick her up from school in case of an emergency. Isola panicked at the possibility that she might be in an emergency while her parents were halfway around the world in Europe. Or worse, they might get into an accident over there and miss her tenth birthday and never see her again. How could they think about traveling without her? She was their only child!

"Isola, come here, mija." Her mother stopped her typing and turned toward her. Isola ran into her arms. "It's only going to be for a little bit, one month, that's all." She stroked Isola's long hair.

"But I want to go with you." Isola squeezed her mother's waist, then lightly touched the pencil that fastened her hair into a knot high on her head like a crown.

"You'll have fun here. Gretchen will take you to theater camp at Golden Gate Park. You won't even miss us."

"Yes, I will. And I don't want to go to theater camp or any summer camp."

"Camp is fun. You'll meet new friends and do something other than sit in your room and read." She kissed Isola's cheeks and pulled her bangs away from her eyes.

"But I like reading." Isola let her hair fall over her eyes.

"Then I'm sure you'll find time for reading. You always do." Her mother turned back to her letter.

"But I'd rather go on the trip with you and Papi." Isola sat at the opposite end of the kitchen table, shrugged her shoulders, and let out a long sigh she hoped could be heard from across the bay.

"You won't appreciate Europe until you're older. Remember how you didn't like traveling to México?" Her mother continued to smooth Isola's bangs away from her face. She seemed to be thinking hard, calculating figures in her mind, as if she might tell Isola she could go.

"But Europe and Paris are different," Isola said, thinking she had a chance to change her mother's mind.

"Different, further away, and more expensive." Her mother still had her thinking-hard expression.

"You said the camp was expensive." Isola tried to make her voice sound deep like her father's, with lots of "authority," her mother's new word.

"Not as expensive as a plane ticket to London. You can stay at Gretchen's and not go to camp, but you can't come with us, young lady."

Isola hated hearing "young lady;" the words always meant her mother was being serious and stubborn. Isola retreated to her room. Maybe if she sulked until it was time for her parents to leave, they'd change their minds and take her with them. Then she had a better idea than pouting. Her mother might swat her fanny with her chancla, but it was worth risking because her mother never hit her very hard, especially since she favored the same old sandals that were soft and floppy. She'd at least show her mother how desperately she wanted to go. She had already tried winning Papi over, but he insisted that her mother was the one who worried about not having enough spending money for their trip if they brought her along. She promised him until she was blue in the face that if they took her with them, she wouldn't ask for anything or whine or complain. She was dying to see Paris and Grandma Palan in Poland. He told her to talk to her mother, but his strategy wasn't helping. She ran back to the kitchen and pulled the sheet from the typewriter. Her mother's face seemed surprised, as if Isola had magically turned into a unicorn. However, her mother managed to snatch the letter back from Isola's loose grasp. In one swift motion, her mother set the letter down and removed her Birkenstock and whacked Isola on her behind. "Traviesa, that's not going to help. Wait until I tell Papi what you've done!" She crumpled the letter and threw it in the wastebasket. Her mother's darkened face said enough. She put her sandal back on, stood tall, and pointed with her whole arm extended until Isola went to her room and slammed the door.

"What did I tell you about slamming my doors?"

"Isola, how you exaggerate! You know I wouldn't do that to my tenants. There you go with your barking."

"That was my mom's thing. You know I don't bark. You used to be so nice to me."

"But you're family. You know that." Gretchen moved closer to Isola.

"Still, you could've asked me first," Isola said.

"You're right, mija. I made a mistake. I shouldn't have assumed. I apologize." Gretchen ran her fingers through her curly gray bob. She stared down at her white house slippers and pulled up her thick socks.

Isola looked up at Gretchen. Despite her girth, Gretchen appeared diminutive, a shadow of her stronger self. Thick crescents of folded skin below her pale blue eyes made Gretchen's whole face appear worried. Did she always have such severe bags? She must be really sorry. Isola had never heard the word "sorry" from Gretchen or her mother. She felt bad for making Gretchen's face darken and sag with hurt. Isola wiped away a new stream of tears.

"Can't I keep the apartment until I sort everything out? I'll be quick, a few months."

"Do you have to be so selfish? You with an apartment and two houses and my brother here from Germany."

"I didn't see it that way. It's just that all my stuff is here and I'm already clearing out the house in Arizona. It's too much right now."

"You never see things other people's way; that's your problem."

Isola fell silent. Gretchen's words carried a special meaning, as if she had been hearing them all her life in a language she didn't understand. Isola allowed herself to consider how selfish she was being and had always been.

"I'm going to call Mrs. Sánchez, grab a few things, make some other phone calls, and then fly back to Phoenix tomorrow."

"Tomorrow? You just got here. You can stay longer." Gretchen washed her mug in the sink and dried it with a dish towel that she had brought from her apartment.

"No, there's too much to take care of at that house and I want to ge over with." Isola walked toward the bay window. The view was ama' She'd hate to give up the apartment, but knew Gretchen would force

15

What She Didn't Say

San Francisco, CA, 1997

Isola awoke to her favorite view of the Bay Bridge peeking beyond gray fog. Books and bags that most likely belonged to Gretchen's brother were scattered by the leather sofa. She hadn't been dreaming. Her head ached at the thought of Gretchen and the liberties she took. Isola was so tired and groggy she didn't notice the stack of mail that Gretchen had plopped on the nightstand either last night or early this morning.

Coffee. Before anything else happened, Isola needed coffee. She started a pot and went back to her letters. Gretchen had filtered out all her junk mail. She found the two envelopes the old woman had made such a fuss about. The letters had been hastily opened. Gretchen hadn't bothered to use steam or stealth. Wasn't tearing into someone else's mail a crime anymore?

Isola picked up the smaller envelope with a handwritten address. The letter was from Mrs. Sánchez, the woman who rented the converted garage behind her mother's San Francisco house. She was asking Isola about *her* intentions for the house and for the apartment. Isola's thoughts went fuzzy. What does she want from me?

Isola put the letter down and poured herself a mug of strong coffee. The nutty aroma reminded her of when she had first heard of Mrs. Sánchez. After her father died, her mother had cleared out the garage to rent to a single woman and had taken a liking to Mrs. Sánchez, a widow. The coffee worked its magic and Isola began to feel more human and sane. She didn't have to reread the letter to have the words sink in and make sense. Mrs. Sánchez was concerned about Isola's plans for the house because she was moving in with her son and wasn't sure the new arrangement would work out. She mentioned that the move was temporary, only until she recovered from her hip replacement surgery. She didn't want to become a burden to her son. She wanted to know if she'd have the option to move back to the place she had called home for so many years. My plans? Isola had assumed her mother had sold the house. Was I wrong all this time? It can't be mine. Can it? She realized how foolish she had been in ignoring all of the requests from lawyers to meet with her. They had important information to give her but her depression had taken over and she'd snubbed them all. No wonder Liz Martínez found her childish. She had been ignoring a great responsibility, and as the lawyer said, stood to inherit a great deal of money. She had a feeling she'd at last be able to pay off her student loans.

The second letter containing instructions from the house's title company confirmed Mrs. Sánchez's assumption. Sharp pangs of pain and regret coursed straight to Isola's heart. Mamá had put her first all along. She really loved me, Isola thought. Her mother had also left Isola the house in San Francisco. She had left nothing to her sister Bernarda or any of her nieces or nephews. She wondered if Gretchen knew of her mother's intentions to leave her everything. Isola vowed to do something for her aunt and cousins. She hadn't heard from Manuelita or her aunt Bernarda in several years.

The door creaked open. Gretchen let herself in.

"I'm such an idiot," Isola said. Hot stinging tears ran down her cheeks. Her sobs became louder and uncontrollable.

The thought that her mother had left her the house in Arizona *and* the house in San Francisco brought on a fresh new stream of tears.

"I didn't know," Isola said. "All this time I didn't know." She wiped her face with the back of her hand.

"It's OK." Gretchen patted Isola's back and stroked her hair. Isola collapsed into Gretchen's soft arms.

"I was so resentful. I thought she had sold the house when she moved to Arizona." Isola extracted herself from Gretchen's suffocating embrace.

"That's what she let us believe. But your mother never said the truth exactly." Gretchen sighed.

"Why was she always saying the opposite of what she meant?" Isola blew her nose. "I never understood that about her."

Gretchen shrugged her shoulders. "I came to offer you som I see you've made some."

"Thank you. Sit down. Do you want some?"

Gretchen nodded. Isola knew Gretchen liked her coffee.

"When I read the letter I didn't understand why you we greedy in keeping the two houses and my apartment." She look before sipping her coffee.

"I haven't intentionally been greedy. You know me. I hon have much cash. It may look like I've inherited a big estate, but I haven't seen any of the money. Despite your generous discount for ment, it's still expensive to live in San Francisco. Plus, I didn't get

"You didn't want the job." Gretchen looked her in the eye.

"I'm a mess. I couldn't seriously consider the job. What, fly forth from here to Arizona?"

"You managed to make it back so quickly."

"This all started with you opening my mail." Isola put her har hips, tapped her foot, and tried to sound serious, but a laugh escap

"If I hadn't opened those letters you wouldn't know important i tion about your fellowship, about the probate in Arizona, about the c of Mrs. What's-her-face."

"Sánchez," Isola said. "Mrs. Carmen Sánchez," Isola repeated more

"I hear you." Gretchen clanked her cup on the thick glass table

"Don't change the subject. I'm serious. You could've told me yo going to have your brother stay at my place." Isola gathered the ba weren't hers and put them by Gretchen's feet. "These belong to your br

"Not that again. When I called, you said you were going to s Arizona and that you couldn't get away. I would've worked somethin out." Gretchen poured herself more coffee.

Isola watched Gretchen go to her refrigerator and help herself to c for her coffee. Apparently Gretchen had also bought groceries for her br to use in her apartment. She was still annoyed Gretchen hadn't first tho to have them stay in her own extra room.

"Like what? Put them in Gina's apartment? Then we'll see whose v she'll be banging on." Isola's voice rose again. She banged on the wall in ame way Gina did to complain when Isola was being too loud.

leave now that she was no longer a starving student and she had her brother and his wife to take care of.

"I wish I could help you, but you know how I feel about flying. My nerves can't take it." Gretchen trembled and crossed herself.

"I know. You can help me with the house here. I want to keep the San Francisco house."

"I will. You'll have plenty of help. Don't worry. I'm sure Renée will come and your other friends from school."

"Renée just says she wants to help . . ." Isola's words trailed off. She looked out the window. She heard shuffling and the door close. Gretchen had left her alone, but had sneaked something onto the table, an ocotillo dreams card. Isola could recognize her mother's favorite postcard a mile away, *Welcome to Chandler, AZ, Where Ocotillo Dreams Come True*. As usual, her mother had been brief. Writing only a single sentence: "How are you, mija?" I need you, Isola thought.

16

Alberto's Taquería

Nacho chopped lettuce and tomatoes in the back of Alberto's Taquería. A thin stream of smoke from a tall candle with the image of the Virgin of Guadalupe blessed the room. The workers in the front room spooned pinto beans, meat, rice, along with Nacho's finely chopped lettuce strips onto large olla-sized tortillas. A customer's no-sour-cream mix-up helped Nacho decide on what to choose for his lunch break. He sat on a concrete block under a small tarp and didn't notice the big guy standing before him as he lapped up the mess of sour cream oozing down his arm. Nacho looked up and saw his manager standing before him.

"¿Jesús?"

"¿Sí, jefe?" Nacho said.

"It's your lucky day. And I'm not talking about your free lunch." The manager slapped Nacho's back, spilling the Styrofoam cup balanced between his knees. "Your mica checks out. You have the job."

Nacho stood up and shook the manager's hand. He was still chewing as the manager continued to explain the position.

"Alberto's is a respectable eatery. We provide housing for all our employees, but you must follow the rules. ¿Comprende?"

For Nacho, the news was like winning the lottery. His daily prayers to the Virgin of Guadalupe had paid off. He was going to get five dollars and fifty cents an hour. He finished chewing, wiped his hands, and thanked the manager again.

"La migra picked up Pedrito, and the boss doesn't want to hire anybody without papers."

"¡Gracias, jefe!" Nacho said.

"Pick up your keys at this address after you leave and memorize these rules." The manager handed Nacho a folded piece of paper, the address and rules barely legible through the stains and creases.

He started yelling out each rule as if Nacho couldn't read in English or Spanish, "Number one, tenants must ask for permission to paint walls. Number two, front doors must be locked at all time." Nacho followed as the manager read. He mouthed each rule to himself.

When the manager got to the tenth rule, "No guests or non-employees allowed in your apartment. Only approved family members with identification and proof of relationship," the manager repeated himself twice and emphasized each word slowly. Nacho tried to make eye contact with him and wanted to laugh, but was too disturbed by the man's serious voice. He knew he couldn't let any of his friends stay there, not Cruz or any of his cousins. The dishwasher and the cooks had already warned him. They suspected Pedrito had been caught with a woman in the apartment, and not by la migra, as they had wanted everyone to believe. Nacho didn't understand what the big deal was, but he wasn't about to ask any questions.

"Do you understand rule ten? I'm serious about not bringing anyone to the apartments, especially anyone without papers. The last thing señor Alberto needs is to have his restaurant shut down by la migra. They'll come and take all of you to jail, green card or no. ¿Comprende?"

"Sí, jefe."

They shook hands once again and Nacho went back to chopping lettuce.

Nacho grew sick of the smell of sour cream after his first day working lettuce at Alberto's. He was grateful for the job that offered him housing. Anything was better than his aunt's house. Alberto's apartment complex was close enough to hitch a ride or take the bus to all his hangouts. No more handouts from Tía Trini and no more crawling through doggy doors or sleeping on other people's hammocks. As long as he could chop lettuce, he would have his own place to sleep. He held the blue ticket tightly in his fingers. The copy of Alberto's rules was tucked in his back pocket. He stood in front of the door before he finally knocked. No one answered. He waited five more minutes before trying the door and entering.

Bunk beds topped with laundry sacks lined the living room entrance. The apartment smelled of sour milk and dirty clothes. He heard no "hello" or "who the hell are you" from the few occupants inside. Nacho walked past the living room and kitchen to a small hallway, blindly turning to the left, then to the right where the narrow corridor opened onto another bedroom with boy-sized bunk beds. The lower bunk, stripped bare, had a number that matched the one on his ticket.

No need for staying in the apartment, he thought. It was 7:30 p.m. and time to meet Cruz for a beer. Nacho took one last look around the apartment before heading out. He opened the refrigerator and heard a loud flush from the bathroom; heavy footsteps followed the noise of a slammed door.

"¿Nombre?" The man said.

"Nnn . . . Jesús." Nacho quickly remembered to say his given name.

"Where's your paper?"

"You mean this?" Nacho handed the man the blue ticket.

"I'm Gabriel, the room leader. You have the bed in the back."

Gabriel opened the refrigerator door and stuck his head in. He pointed to the empty space on the bottom shelf and told Nacho he could keep his food there.

"Here's your key. Don't make a copy and don't give it to anyone else or you'll be kicked out of the job and the apartment."

Nacho nodded. Gabriel left without saying more. The mattress and pillow were stained. Nacho would have to ask Trini for some bedding.

17

Nacho's Luck

By the time Cruz made it to Rosie's Restaurant, Nacho and his sister had already started on tacos and beer, and Epifanía was ready to dance to the ranchera playing on the jukebox. The big smile on Nacho's face made him look drunk. Cruz ordered a beer and waited for Nacho to spill his good news. Nacho always smiled like a happy, drunken loco when he had good news.

"I got in at Alberto's." Nacho tilted his chair back and rocked forward with a thud that shook their table.

"I can smell the news on you." Cruz sniffed at Nacho's armpits, then rubbed his belly. "You smell like a taco, good enough to eat."

"Get away from me, cabrón." Nacho threw a soft jab at Cruz's arm. "I was going to put in a good word for you too, ese."

"Stop that. Finish my plate for me." Epifanía shoved her food in front of Cruz. He loved the way she was always caring for others.

Cruz knew Pifi preferred to date Anglos, men with money. But he'd never forget the one night Pifi was too drunk to say no to him. She'd cooked him chorizo and eggs the next morning and kissed him one last time before kicking him out of her patrona's house and making him swear on the death of his mother not to tell Trini or Nacho. She can be such a baby sometimes, he thought. Other times she was exactly like his mother, making sure he ate and fussing over him.

"Mi tía says you are working days and nights, too." Pifi seemed worried. "Is it true?"

"Thanks to her, no. She won't even give me a scrap of rug to sleep on. No, hombre. I had this plan to work at nights, but she doesn't even listen to my ideas."

"Don't take it personally. She barely talks to us." Pifi let loose her pony tail and fluffed her long, thick hair. "You are invited to our fiesta next Sunday. Trini said to tell you."

"No. After the other day, I cannot show my face at her door."

"Just come." Pifi patted his back.

"Trini expects us to provide the meat and the beer. She won't care if you show up with a six-pack." Nacho swallowed his last bite and licked the grease from his wrists.

"Ingratos, both of you! Trinidad is more than generous." Pifi finished her beer. "So if you didn't sleep at my tía's, pues, ¿dónde dormiste, con tu novia?"

"Me? I hear the fruncido Anglo you go out with made you pay for his ticket to the show, and so did your other boyfriend, Chato."

"What did my tía tell you? Chato's my cousin. And you? Crying over that vendida Rosalina." Epifanía darted him a look of pure evil.

"Cut it out!" Nacho slammed his beer down. "What's up with you? You've been starting pleito from the moment you walked in."

"No, I haven't. She's talking about my brother's wife." Cruz wondered why women were so jealous of each other. In his mind, Rosalina was the purest and most beautiful of all women. He would have married her if his older brother hadn't stolen her from him. Even to this day, he only wanted happiness for Rosalina. What he couldn't understand was why Nacho was taking his sister's side. He never did that.

"I just want to enjoy my beer without you two getting started." Nacho pushed the tall cup away.

"When I go home, I'll give that vendida a piece of my mind." Pifi leaned in close to Cruz.

"¿Vendida? What kind of talk is that? Rosalina never did anything to you. She was always nice to you and you liked her," Cruz said. "You always preferred hanging around with the guys than being friends with a nice girl like Rosalina."

"Nice girl? The sinvergüenza married her boyfriend's brother and never returned my huipil, the one I was supposed to get married in." Epifanía blurted out her venom as the waitress cleared their plates and wiped the table.

"Who would marry a woman with your mouth?" Cruz said. "I can't imagine you giving Rosalina a huipil or a white wedding dress." He raised his glass to order another beer. "You don't even wear skirts. You're always in those tight jeans."

"Mentiroso, like you know my whole wardrobe." Her words rose above the music. "What else do you know about me?"

"¿Y tú?" Epifanía turned toward Nacho and gave him her evil stare. "What are you looking at?" Nacho gestured with raised hands. He was staying out of the fight.

Cruz stared hard at her. He didn't want to tell her what he was really thinking. "What I really want to know is how you cross back and forth all the time. All this started because you said you were going home to cuss out Rosalina, an innocent." He slammed his glass on the table.

"She's la migra's puta." Nacho's laugh died quickly. He seemed to regret talking that way about his little sister.

"You better take that back or I will tell Mamá." Epifanía smacked her brother with her damp napkin.

"I take it back. I take it back." Nacho raised his arms in surrender.

"I'm going to change the music." Pifi walked over to the jukebox.

"So, where did you sleep if not at Trini's?" Nacho's shiny teeth seemed to know the answer.

"At the empty house. The daughter told me to stay."

"¡Uh que la chingada! You're in for trouble." Nacho smiled his wide smile.

Epifanía let out a huffy sigh. She seemed to have heard every word as she made her request of Freddy Fender's "Wasted Days and Wasted Nights."

Cruz recalled the long talk he and Nacho had had about not getting involved with doña Marina's daughter. He recalled the many conversations he had had with Marina herself about her daughter.

He wanted to confide in Nacho and tell him how torn he was about staying at doña Marina's house now that her daughter was there alone, but he didn't think Nacho would understand his feelings for Isola. How vulnerable and sad and alone Isola had seemed. He felt obligated to stay because Isola had practically begged him to. Cruz chose not to say anything. He didn't want to share Isola with Nacho or Epifanía or anyone.

He knew that whatever he said wouldn't matter. Epifanía would continue with her frown and Nacho would taunt him with the smile he reserved for moments he thought himself better than the rest of the world. Today Nacho got a job at Alberto's. His big toothy grin made him seem as though he'd soar above the restaurant and land flat on the moon to shine his big white smile back to Cruz on Earth. Nacho had all the luck and big ears for hearing about good jobs.

Cruz envied Nacho's luck, but was more sorry about losing his friend and partner to Nacho's job at Alberto's. Nacho had helped Cruz find jobs and places to sleep. Life was easy with his childhood friend at his side. The two worked well together and he'd often put in a good word for him at doña Trini's. Alberto's was one of the best jobs in all of Phoenix. He didn't doubt his friend had tried to put in a good word for him. There was free food and housing, and the pay was good. That kind of treatment was unheard of in México. Nacho had the advantage of speaking better English than he did, but he didn't need any skills to cut lettuce, and that's what Nacho said he did all day. Cruz prayed for another position to become available at Alberto's; he wouldn't have to worry about where to spend the night and he wouldn't be tempted by doña Marina's beautiful daughter. However, Cruz aspired to do more than making burritos and cutting lettuce for a taquería. He wondered if Isola would help him get a better job.

"Are you having another Corona?" Nacho said.

"No." Cruz stood up and excused himself. "I have work early in the morning."

"We know what kind of work." Epifanía high-fived her brother. They laughed and followed Cruz out.

"Put in a word for me at Alberto's," Cruz yelled from the parking lot.

Nacho lifted his chin and waved. "You need a ride? Pifi borrowed a car."

"No." Cruz hollered back. "I'll take the bus."

Cruz's answer made Epifanía and Nacho start up another round of laughter.

"Ven-di-da!" Epifanía yelled as Cruz hopped on the bus.

18

Quiet Moment

The sounds of the cantina's jukebox and Epifanía's laughter seemed far away after Cruz closed his eyes and settled in on the clean sheets Isola had put on the couch. Isola told him to use her bed while she was away, but he insisted the couch would be good enough for him. The two days he had spent alone in the house felt like a dream. Cruz not only had a comfortable place to stay, but several rooms to himself and the swimming pool and money in his pocket for the easy task of helping a beautiful woman move boxes and haul trash. Isola had paid him generously for helping her organize the house. He kept finding extra bills tucked into his jeans and shirt pockets. He unfolded the two hundreds Isola had given him and placed them in his wallet. Save your money, he told himself. Save. His dream life with Isola wasn't going to last long and he wanted to do a better job of setting himself up than he had done with doña Marina, who hadn't offered to give him the mica. Marina had been good to him, but was more loyal to her friends. She had wanted Josefina to have the mica for her cholito nephew who didn't deserve the ID or the birth certificate. He tossed and turned on the sofa and started counting backwards, but nothing seemed to help his restlessness. His wristwatch said 3:30 a.m. when he decided to put his own affairs in order. He opened his backpack and refolded his change of clothes and put the pants and shirt on the table. He zipped the money envelope inside one of the backpack's compartments. Save your money, he repeated. Save.

The next envelope he took out made him feel hot and anxious. He felt a cloud of guilt choke him, as if the hand of God were intervening. As soon as he thought about returning the papers to Marina's file box, the choking cloud disappeared. However, his guilt was not strong enough to force him to return the papers to Isola. He took the papers out of the envelope and unfolded Marcel Palan's birth certificate and his identification card. Isola had been searching for her father's documents all week. He had found them this morning in one of the boxes Isola hadn't gone through. He reminded himself he had better use for the papers than a punk kid. A stronger pinch of guilt pricked the back of his neck as he thought about his betrayal of Marina. "Disrespecting a deceased woman's wishes is bad luck," his mother had once told him. He'd risk a little bad luck because the mica would solve all his problems. He told himself it had been his good fortune to find the envelope with the papers Isola had been looking so hard for. He wanted to do the right thing and let the choice be hers, but was convinced that she'd never let him have the papers no matter how much she cared for him or enjoyed his company.

Cruz still didn't understand why Isola had gone on a last-minute trip to San Francisco. Her crazy trip had also been a miracle. The time alone in the house gave him a chance to think and get organized. She was too young, too smart, too beautiful for him. "It won't last," he told himself as he folded the birth certificate and tucked it back in the envelope. He hid the identification card in his wallet behind a card that had spaces for his name, address, and telephone number. Deep inside he refused to believe his relationship with Isola would last. More important, he didn't think he deserved happiness with a woman like Isola. Betrayal was inevitable, he thought. However, he wished there were another way. "God forgive me," he whispered. He knew Isola would never forgive him. "I have to do this," he reminded himself.

The first thing he had to do was figure out who he could trust to alter the documents so that he could use them. He hoped the two hundred dollars would cover the cost of changing a few details on the birth certificate and driver's license. He had heard enough stories about people stealing the money and mica and leaving the poor vato to bleed to death from a knife wound. At least these were from a man already dead, he rationalized. He was confident he'd find one good person to help him out, either Nacho or one of Nacho's cousins. Cruz knew it was useless to think about all the stories he had heard of mica deals gone bad. He zipped up his belongings in the green canvas backpack and closed his eyes. He had been lucky so far. Someone's looking out for me.

He awoke after an hour and reread Marina's letter to Josefina and thought twice about destroying the letter. What difference did it make? She already knows Marina had left the mica to Josefina. Isola had so few letters and memories of her mother. He put the letter back in the file and felt better about himself, less guilty. He thought Isola should have the letter since she was not going to find the mica. Would she suspect he had the mica if she found the letter? Better not think of that. She acted like a wild woman at the mention of her father's papers. The one time he had jokingly asked her to give them to him, if she ever found them, she practically bit his head off. Cruz swore she had even barked at him. There was no other choice. He knew he'd be risking everything if she found out that he had taken the papers. He tugged at his long sideburns. Don't do it, don't do it. But it was far too tempting. With the papers, he'd have more opportunities and get better jobs than Nacho or Epifanía, who thought she was so big cleaning houses. Cruz continued to convince himself that for all of Isola's frustrations over her father's papers, he could count on her playfulness and good nature. He loved how easy it was to make her laugh and stop taking herself so seriously.

The sun started to rise in the horizon and the sky lightened from midnight blue to violet. Cruz grabbed a towel from the bathroom and stripped. The coolness of the morning tickled the hairs on his chest and arms. He waded into the pool slowly and allowed the surprise of the cold water to awaken him. He swam ten laps, slicing through the water effortlessly. The crisp clapping noise of his lone strokes in the water were paradise. He listened to the quiet of the neighborhood, so much more peaceful than doña Trini's. Cruz meditated on the quiet, pondered the silence as if morning solitude were a new invention. He ignored his sore muscles and lifted himself out of the pool like an athlete, catapulting himself to standing. He toweled off, stretched, and resisted the urge to belt out a huge grito to announce his presence in the world. He had never known such freedom, such privacy to walk around in the backyard naked. Having such a big house to himself, without sneaking around, gave him a glimpse of what it must be like to be an American.

Sparrows awakened and began their song. For the first time, he allowed himself to think of Marina and the last trip they had made together in the desert. She hadn't complained about the heat or being tired or anything. At the time, he had no idea she had cancer. He was amazed by how Marina had hidden her cancer and how ill she was. During her last days, Marina had never ceased helping people cross the border and offering them shelter until they got onto their own feet. His thoughts drifted to Isola and he felt sorry for her loss—and his.

Inside he drank a glass of milk and a glass of orange juice before catching the six a.m. bus to Mesa. University students reading books and newspapers sat at the front. Cruz took a seat at the back of the bus. He closed his eyes for a few minutes, but the sunlight was too strong. Instead, he gazed enviously at the drivers in their cars on their way to work. A woman in a silver car was putting on her makeup, her hands barely touching the steering wheel. Cruz vowed to save money for a car. Doña Marina had long ago given her car away to a friend of Josefina's. Marina must've known how sick she was to have given the car away to someone she hadn't known very well. Cruz was disappointed she hadn't left him the car.

The bus crossed Tempe, dropped off the university students, and turned onto the highway for one exit before reaching la barda. Cruz saw the familiar faces he hadn't seen during the week he had spent with Isola. The men lined up in front of the mini mart, some found shade beside the side of the building, some squatted underneath a sparse tree, but most waited on the front sidewalk. The hungrier ones walked across the block to catch the trucks before they pulled up. Cruz never recognized the drivers. The cars and jobs were always different. So much work and opportunity. Cruz thought of home, his favorite daydream and pastime.

"Hermano," an old man called to Cruz in a raspy voice. Cruz was pulled away from his daydream of Atlixco's colorful plaza and bright tiled fountain in the placita's center.

He turned and saw a familiar face. As he walked toward him, he remembered the man Elorio, who had given him the idea of sleeping during the day and working at night. How doña Trini had laughed at this idea and danced around like a clown. He should know better than to take suggestions from strangers. What did this old man know anyway? He seemed too old for work. Cruz wondered why Elorio spent his time at la barda. His brown work pants and dark green shirt were clean, but his dark gray hair seemed greasy, as if he never washed it.

"Did you find work with my nephew at the telephone company? Did you ask for Miguel Murillo?" Up close, Elorio didn't look so old.

"No," Cruz said. "I thought about it, but I decided to stick with day jobs."

"It's not for everybody." Elorio pointed to the van approaching. A red truck honked at the men. Cruz turned and took a step toward the van, but saw that it was already full. "Ey, does this mean you're not having trouble finding places to stay?"

Cruz shrugged. The man must sense he has money, Cruz thought. Two men seated near the mini mart listened in on his conversation. He didn't like the attention the hard-of-hearing man brought with his loud voice. Cruz waved to him and started to walk away.

"Oye, espera." Elorio hopped off the concrete bench and put a hand on Cruz's shoulder. "I have a friend who needs a place to stay. You seem to be doing well for yourself."

"I'm not any better off than I was last week, hermano," Cruz raised his voice for the benefit of the two men listening to him.

"Can you help my friend?" Elorio lowered his voice. Cruz sensed the "friend" he was talking about was himself. He felt sorry for Elorio and a little guilty about all the rooms he had to himself, the mica, and the envelope of cash, which he told himself he'd better put in a bank. However, his feeling of guilt floated away, and Cruz didn't think he owed anything to Elorio. All the man had offered him was a crazy scheme about working at night and sleeping during the day. He didn't even know if the man actually had a nephew who worked at the phone company. Maybe someone else had told him of the scheme. Something told him not to trust him. He thought about all the breaks strangers had given him in Arizona, but Cruz was wary. He wasn't going to help someone he didn't know. He had a hard enough time taking care of himself and getting ahead.

"No, I can't help your friend." Cruz pictured strangers moving in on the house, on Isola. He vowed not to tell anyone of the empty house.

"But he, my friend, is related to my nephew's sister." Elorio's pleas sounded more desperate. He rubbed his hands as though he were creating magic.

Cruz studied Elorio's hands, lined with thick green veins. "Lo siento," Cruz said. He wasn't going to take any chances. The next van approached and Cruz was the first inside. He didn't care where it was going or what kind of work he was needed to do. His heart raced from the sprint and his back was beginning to feel damp. At twenty-seven, he felt too old to be running after work. Tomorrow he'd try to get work at Thornton; maybe he'd enroll in English classes at the city college.

19

Desert Heat

Isola stepped out of the cab and paid the driver. The full force of the desert's heat nearly evaporated her memory of the short time she had spent in San Francisco. She remembered how to breathe in the convection-oven air that felt as if her innards were being slow-cooked with each inhalation. As she made her way to the shade of the garage, she was glad she had changed into flip-flops and a sundress. Her suitcase tires made crunching noises over the concrete driveway. She wondered why the garage door was wide open.

Cruz came into the garage carrying one of her mother's boxes, the ones she had so carefully sifted through before her trip. Cruz added the box to the row against the wall and tidied the line of boxes. Isola stacked her tote and her bags on top of her suitcase and rushed up to Cruz, who extended his arms in grand gesture of his accomplishment.

"What are you doing? I had those boxes organized. I'm going to have to start over again." She rested her fists on her hips and looked away from Cruz while she waited for his explanation.

Cruz didn't say anything for several seconds. He hung his head and looked as though he would've stuck his tail between his legs too, if he had one. Isola realized she had used her angry-teacher voice. She didn't mean to be so dramatic.

She continued to wait while he hung his head and looked as though he were about to cry. She was going to faint if she stayed, waiting for Cruz to speak in the saunalike garage. She didn't think her tone had been so severe.

"I'm waiting." Isola put her face in front of Cruz and tried to get him to smile. She was surprised by how hard it was to maintain a serious tone with Cruz; she was genuinely happy to see him again. He continued to wear his hurt look.

"You are going to get mad again." Cruz walked inside the house.

"OK, what else am I going to be mad at?" Isola followed Cruz into the living room.

"También limpié la piscina." Cruz pointed to the sparkling pool. She noticed he had also cleaned the dusty mini blinds and the large window.

"Don't you want to go outside?" Cruz said.

"Thanks, but I don't care if you cleaned out the swimming pool. I'm talking about the boxes from upstairs. I was looking for some very important papers."

"I did not disturb the papers inside the boxes. I only stacked the boxes against the wall, aquí. I wanted to help you." Cruz continued to wear his sad eyes.

She liked the way his turquoise T-shirt made his eyes stand out. His brown eyes calmed her. They were like her father's eyes, smooth chestnut shells. She remembered when Grandma Palan had told her that her father had inherited her mother's Mexican genes and that he was more like her, of the Mexican Ibarra line, than of her husband's Polish Palan side. She called her son her "coffee bean" because his skin was darker than her own, "robust and hardy," not like her husband's delicate porcelain skin that burned on a cloudy day. Grandma Palan's chestnut eyes always seemed fiery when she talked about all things Mexican. Isola had a hard time remembering her grandmother's voice. The sound and pitch of her voice escaped her, even though they had often talked on the telephone before she died. But she remembered how lonely Grandma Palan had been in Poland. Grandma Palan adored Marina and loved to tell the story of how her son had fallen in love with a beautiful Mexican woman in San Francisco. Everyone had loved Marina. Isola had always felt insignificant in her mother's shadow. She was the lonely speck of dust left in the wind with Papá and Grandma Palan gone, and now both her parents too.

She thought about how she had left her problems and a house in disarray on Cruz. She had accepted his help and shouldn't fault him for trying to please her. "I'm sorry. I'm not angry at you. I know you were trying to help me, but those boxes represent clues to my mother's life. Do you realize how important they are? Anything from that pile, I need you to leave to me to sort. I should've made that clear before I left." Isola blurted out the words in one long breath.

Cruz seemed even smaller and more dejected than when she first reprimanded him and didn't seem to understand everything she was saying. "It's OK. But don't help me unless I ask you to because I can't organize anything if you keep undoing the progress that I've made." She didn't feel like translating. "No tengas pena. It's fine. Just leave the boxes upstairs for me to sort. Agreed?"

"Agreed." Cruz repeated her and shook her hand.

Isola threw her arms around him. Cruz welcomed her closeness. He folded her into him and caressed the small of her back. The hug felt good. It had been a long time since a man had touched her in the space between her back and buttocks, the place for slow dancing. His hand behind her waist was even more electrifying than when she had first met him and he respectfully took her palm in his. She pulled away from her exuberance of forgiving, feeling both sorry the hug was over and strangely confused that she had initiated the awkward exchange.

Cruz walked past the living room and put his hand on the doorknob. He curled his finger and beckoned Isola to follow him. She didn't trust the strange expression on his face. When she didn't budge, he took her arm and loosely covered her eyes while he opened the door to the backyard. Outside, she saw he had planted fresh flowers and had pulled out several patches of weeds. The yard was beautiful. She gasped and pressed her folded hands to her chest. The former pond of scum and algae was now a sparkling, inviting pool. Cruz removed his shoes and shirt. He gave her a sideways glance, the look a child gives before he's about to create some mischief.

"You're not up to any funny business now. Are you?"

Cruz nodded yes and crept toward her like Frankenstein's monster.

"Oh, no you don't!" She stepped back from him.

"Sí, sí, sí." He lunged and grabbed her arm, seized her torso, flung her into the pool, and jumped in behind her.

Isola's flip-flops floated to the surface. Her loose white cotton dress ballooned like a lotus blossom. She relaxed after the initial shock of the cold water. Swimming was not an activity she normally indulged in. Cruz flipped his hair away from his eyes. She moved to the shallow end to where her tiptoes touched the bottom. She didn't know what to do next. She was too nervous to move. Cruz watched her. She swam a lap and circled back to the middle of pool. Cruz caught up with her and surprised her with a kiss. She didn't pull away. They kissed and held each other in a long embrace. His wet kiss was invigorating. Her body tingled. She felt awake and alive, elated to feel something other than grief, anger, and frustration. The kiss made her feel light as Fairy Queen Mab of dreams. She kissed him again before Cruz helped her up the steps.

He handed her a towel. She wrapped it around her dripping dress. Cruz showed off his other surprise. He had stacked up towels in the cabana and had prepared the grill.

"Very nice! You've been keeping busy." She dried her hair with the towel. "Oh, I forgot. I brought something for you." Isola ran inside.

She returned and saw that Cruz had quickly peeled off his jeans and put on a dry pair. "Here, it's nothing, it's from the airport."

He fumbled with his belt as she handed him a plastic bag. Cruz pulled out the T-shirt imprinted with a crooked street and colorful buildings crowded in front of a bridge, and *San Francisco* in big block letters at the bottom. Cruz smiled, tore off the tag and put the T-shirt on. "Gracias." He gave Isola a kiss on the cheek. "I have carne asada in the refrigerator." He gave her another kiss, this time on the lips. "The food will be ready in half an hour."

"Enough time for me to shower." She went back inside. Cruz followed her.

"Déjame," he said. He grabbed her suitcase and hauled it to the top of the stairs. He carried it high above his head, showing off his brawn.

"Thank you." She curtsied and gathered the rest of her bags. Cruz went outside to tend to his grilling. Isola danced up the stairs, taking them two at a time, then falling back a step. She extended her arm with a flourish and blew kisses in Cruz's direction. He couldn't see her and that made her game all the more silly and satisfying.

She emerged in the kitchen wearing bright lipstick and a short red dress she had brought back from San Francisco. The designer dress was much too fancy for wearing around the house, but Isola enjoyed the silky feel of the fabric and the dress's slimming effect on her hips and stomach.

She was touched that Cruz had spent part of the money she had paid him buying flowers for the backyard and groceries for her. It reminded her of how different he was from her ex-boyfriend. Jeremy had always been so penurious, even though he was never poor or starving; he would never have spent money on flowers for her apartment. Cruz was a good guy, she thought. He could get a little carried away when he clowned around, but he was fun. Unlike Jeremy, whose idea of a good time was to invite her to play the video games he knew she hated. She wondered how she had put up with Jeremy for so long.

"The meat will be ready soon," Cruz yelled from the back yard.

She walked in front of the window and waved to Cruz. He took a second look at her dress and she did a little twirl for him. As she took a bow, she heard the doorbell and waltzed toward the door.

Josefina had returned, this time without her nephew.

"¿Tienes fiesta?" Josefina eyed Isola's outfit. Her gaze settled on Isola's fancy shoes.

"No, an early dinner." Isola felt ridiculous in her gold high heels and short silk dress.

"I only wanted to bring you something. I did not know if you were here." Josefina wore a simple brown cotton dress.

"I'm sorry. I thought I gave you my phone number. Come in."

"Gracias." Josefina seemed reluctant to intrude.

"I haven't found the papers or note for you from my mother, but I'll call if I find something." Isola led her to the couch they had sat at before. She pulled up a chair to face Josefina.

"I want to give you some pictures of Marina." Josefina reached inside her purse and pulled out a packet of photos.

"Thank you." Isola studied the photos.

"Most of these were taken here," Josefina said. "Mira. Here is one with your mother in the dress you wore the other day." Josefina's words trailed to a whisper as she looked up in shock. Her expression soured into a disfiguring look of disgust.

Isola turned and only saw Cruz. She didn't know what had transpired between Cruz and Josefina, but it was obvious Josefina did not like him.

Josefina stood as if to leave. "I see you've met Cruz."

"You know Cruz?"

"I know him." Her humble smile soured into a deep scowl. "What is he doing here?" Josefina pointed at Cruz and scanned the living room as if she had never been in the house before. "Stay away from Cruz." She whispered the words and spoke slowly, as though deciding what more to say. "He's . . ." She held back and didn't finish her thoughts. She felt embarrassed and ashamed that she had taken up so quickly with Cruz and here was Josefina, another person she didn't know very well, practically scolding her as if she were a child. She really wanted Josefina to leave.

"He's my friend," Isola said.

"You have friends here? You don't even know him." She shook her head. She seemed disappointed; her sad, crooked face disapproved. "Did you give him the mica? Is that why you haven't called?" Her sharp voice filled the room.

"What? I told you I haven't found it."

"The mica that doña Marina promised me for Alfonso. No es eso. You don't understand." Josefina swatted the air. She tried communicating with her hands, but she struggled to express herself.

Isola suspected Josefina wanted to say much more. One thing was certain: she didn't like Cruz. "Like I said, I haven't seen the mica or the envelope with your name on it. I'll call you if I find a letter addressed to you." Isola walked to the door and waited for Josefina to take the hint and leave.

Cruz opened the back door. "Is Josefina eating with us?" Isola shook her head and Cruz went back to his grilling.

Josefina turned and looked at Cruz in disgust. "I'm leaving."

"Hold on. There's a few more things we need to talk about so you won't be dropping in on me. Sit down. I'll be right back."

She went outside. "Could you wait here while I finish talking to Josefina?"

"Sí." Cruz seemed hurt.

She rushed back inside. "Josefina?" Josefina must've had her nephew waiting for her in the car.

There was no sign of her in the kitchen or anywhere in the house. It appeared Isola wasn't going to have the satisfaction of reassuring Josefina that despite her appearances of playing house with Cruz, she was genuinely looking for any letters or envelopes her mother may have left and, thanks to Cruz, she was making significant progress in organizing her mother's things.

Her frustration mounted as she contemplated her foolishness at caring what Josefina thought. She needed to settle her mother's estate more for herself than for a strange woman. Her mounting credit card debt from her lawyer's fees and student loans was another thing that weighed heavily on her frazzled mind. It didn't help that she had to turn down a teaching position or that she was too depressed to take the job in the first place.

She turned to see Cruz struggling to open the door while juggling two platters of food and was grateful she had someone to lean on.

"What did she want?" Cruz placed the platter on the kitchen table.

"It has something to do with an envelope for her. You haven't seen anything with her name on it? Have you?"

"No. I didn't look in the boxes," he said.

"I'm sorry. I don't mean to seem ungrateful. I know how hard you've worked to help me."

"I'm not going to even look at those boxes." His face looked hurt again.

"She wanted to give me these." Isola showed him the photos. He smiled at seeing the pictures. "How do you know Josefina?"

"I met her here." He gestured to the living room. "Josefina wanted help for her nephew—English classes for him and help finding him a job."

Isola realized that a lot must've happened in her mother's living room.

"You mean her nephew Alfonso? She said he wanted to work, but I thought he seemed so young." She sank into the couch.

"I don't remember his name. I only saw him once from far away while I was working in the backyard." Cruz walked toward Isola and sat next to her.

"It had to be him." Isola couldn't help wondering why Josefina was so put out by Cruz being there. It was none of her business who she befriended. She put her head on Cruz's shoulder.

"Don't make that face." Cruz stroked her damp hair. "Why did she upset you?"

"I don't know. Let's not talk about her." Isola tried to smile.

"Ven." He offered her his hand and pulled her toward the kitchen.

Cruz pointed proudly to his tall stack of meat. His pride for his grilling made her smile. She liked the way he was willing to make a fool of himself to make her smile. Isola decided not to tell Cruz about Josefina's previous visit and her request for her father's social security card. Or her accusing Isola of giving the card to Cruz. She wasn't going to let Josefina ruin their fun.

"Are you hungry?" Cruz seemed eager to turn her attention to his creation.

"Famished," Isola said. She rubbed her belly and made a sad pout.

Cruz's damp hair smelled of grilled meat. She had a feeling he was serious about his skills with a grill. Cruz laid out meat, beans, tortillas, and salsa. If she hadn't seen him prepare the meal, she would've believed he had ordered the food from a taquería. Cruz rolled a taco and fed it to her. She took a big bite, but avoided touching her lips or tongue to his fingers. He waited for her to chew and gave her a second bite. This time her lips touched his fingers. His fingers lingered on her cheek. She closed her eyes.

"This is really amazing," Isola said with her mouth still full. The food was good, but him making it and feeding it to her was even better.

"It's just carne asada," Cruz said.

"I know, but what did you marinate the meat with?"

Cruz didn't answer her. His eyes met Isola's and he gave her the same mischievous smile he had before he threw her in the pool. His eyes said he was waiting to surprise her again. Isola knew what the surprise was. She smiled too. It was her turn to be mischievous. She was excited by Cruz's anticipation and the way her heartbeat echoed in her stomach. She had never felt such a rush of attraction before. The booming noise in her heart and stomach made her feel as though she were about to burst all her seams with desire. She took his hand and led him to the bedroom upstairs. She quickly flung the red dress off and slid into bed. Cruz's eyes said he was hungry for her. He looked at her as though he had never seen a woman naked before. He took his time unzipping his pants, removing his brand new San Francisco T-shirt, which he took a second glance at before casting it to the floor, on top of Isola's dress. He kept his white underwear on as he pounced on the bed, a jaguar in tidy whites. Isola laughed, grabbed at his underwear, and turned out the light.

Isola awoke to the sound of Cruz's murmurs. She had been sleeping so soundly, she didn't want to turn or awaken from her cocoon of comfort, but the voice she heard sounded gnarled and painful. She leaned her head closer to him, as if trying to breathe in the words he mumbled in his sleep.

Cruz awoke and seemed startled by her face so close to his. He snapped his head and hit his chin against her skull.

"Ay!" Cruz screamed.

They both sat up in bed. Isola switched on the lamp. Cruz held his chin and moved his jaw from side to side.

"¿Qué está pasando?" Cruz said.

"I'm sorry. Did I hurt you?" Isola massaged Cruz's chin. "Are you OK?"

"You scared me. You're the cucuy."

"Don't call me a monster. It's not nice and I didn't mean to scare you. You were having a nightmare. Do you remember what you were dreaming about?" Isola stroked Cruz's chest hair.

"How do you know I was dreaming?" His voice sounded sleepy and groggy.

"You were talking. I tried to hear what you were saying, but the words sounded funny, like you were under water."

"Who talks under water?" Cruz sat up and pretended to speak as if under water. He made big gulping gestures, as if he were swallowing water and talking.

"You know what I mean," she gently shoved him. "Maybe I shouldn't ask," she said. "You cried in your sleep, that's how I found you that first day in the house, remember?"

"Sí." Cruz no longer smiled. He seemed to be elsewhere.

"You don't have to tell me." Isola pressed on his shoulder.

"No. I want to tell you." Cruz took a moment of silence and then a deep breath before he began.

"It's a dream that is very ugly. I'm crossing la frontera. The sun is setting and it's a good time to walk. Farther in the distance I see a woman rocking back and forth, the way somebody tries to quiet a baby. Only the woman does not hold a child. She holds her arms close to her. As I walk toward her, I see she is seated beneath an ocotillo, a skinny cactus with several arms and red flowers at the tip of each branch. The red tips of the ocotillo are covered in blood and drip onto the woman's face. When I reach her, I have a strong feeling that I know her, but I don't recognize her because the blood is covering her face. Despite the blood and her being in the desert, she is singing and she is beautiful. When I see her eyes, I still don't recognize her, but I know

I loved her. Every time I wake up, I taste chocolate in my mouth. I think my tongue is bleeding, but it is not. This time I was not biting on my tongue."

Isola sighed. She carressed Cruz's hair.

"I knew you were a poet," she said.

"It's only a dream."

"It sounds like a story from a fairy tale, the kind your mom reads you when you're a kid."

"My mother never read me fairy tales."

"That's hard to believe."

"Even if she had they wouldn't be as good as the stories my grandmother used to tell me."

"See, we have that in common. We come from a rich culture of storytelling, even though we are so different."

"Sí," Cruz said softly.

"Do you think the dream has something to do with your grandmother's stories?"

"I don't know. But in the dream I feel pure love. The way a grandmother, mother, or a woman loves. I can't explain it."

"You don't have to," Isola said.

She didn't care that he simply repeated a picture dug from the depths of his subconscious. She was moved by his words. His dream reminded her of all the privilege she had grown up with. She thought of her own mother working in the desert, helping people cross the border, and of how her mother died in the land of ocotillos and sand. Cruz's dream had stirred in her every ounce of love she had ever felt. She experienced love piercing her being, a feeling she had long forgotten, that had been buried deep, but resided within her nonetheless. Hearing his dream made her realize her infatuation for Cruz was much deeper than she had allowed herself to believe. She was in love with the man of ocotillo dreams. She'd never think the same again of the desert, of the spindly plant known as the ocotillo, of Cruz.

"Ven." Isola cradled Cruz tightly.

They made love again.

20

A Closer Look

Isola trimmed the wildflowers Cruz had brought her and added water to the slender vase. The bouquet smelled like the desert, earthy and sweet, and she resolved to make their stay at the house more official. With a great show, she pulled on heavy gloves and pulled out the For Sale sign in front of her yard and carried it to the garage. She dusted herself off and looked about the neighborhood to see if anyone was watching. No one saw her big effort, not even Cruz, who was out, she had assumed, trying to prove to her he didn't need her charity. Closed garage doors and shut white miniblinds were her only witnesses in the desert suburb. She pulled up the sign and pushed down all of her worries about the other properties she had to take care of. Gone was all the fuss she had made about her apartment and even further buried was the bigger mess of her mother's San Francisco house. For now, she'd worry about the desert house. "Small chunks" and "baby steps" and "be in the present moment" were her new mantras, but the lingering thought that she had allowed herself to get carried away with her feelings for Cruz brought back the urgency of her need to settle her mother's estate. It had been more than two days since she'd seen Cruz, and she worried he'd given up and gone back home. However, things were going so well and she didn't want to think that something awful might have happened to him. Relax, she told herself. He'll be back. She tried to convince herself that she knew things were OK, but, in truth, she was awfully confused and had no idea where she stood with Cruz.

Chandler, Arizona, was not San Francisco, but it was starting to feel like home. The house now belonged to her, and she had Cruz to thank for putting her back together and removing the stale numbness that had replaced her heart. She knew he wouldn't follow her to the Bay Area, that he'd just as soon give up and go back to México, but she wanted to look after him. She sensed that he was extremely embarrassed about accepting her charity, but she loved taking care of him.

She had started moving more boxes into the garage when Cruz walked in. She turned her back to him and went into the kitchen. She didn't want him to see how hurt she was. They didn't have any rules. He slipped his hands under her arms and hugged her from behind.

"Where were you?" She leaned the back of her head against his chest.

"Trabajando."

"You don't have to take every job that's offered to you. You can do some work here."

"I don't want you to give me everything. I need to find my own work."

"I know." She turned to smell the sweat on his collar.

He kissed the top of her head.

"I was going to shower, then heat up some food. Do you want to shower with me?" she asked. She smiled widely, covered her mouth, and almost laughed.

He seemed confused by her giddy smile.

"No. I'll heat up the food for you while you shower. I just have to use the toilet before you go in to bathe." Cruz turned and took two steps up the stairs.

"Wait!" Isola shouted. "Use the bathroom downstairs."

He looked at her oddly and pointed downstairs, as if they had had a miscommunication.

She could see his brain was working too hard.

"Just go." She shooed him in the direction of the downstairs bathroom.

Isola set the table in the backyard. It was nice to eat outdoors. The nights were so warm. She understood why her mother had preferred the desert to San Francisco. People in Arizona kept to themselves. She thought she'd be hearing more from her neighbors, but she hadn't heard a word from them. Life in the desert was slower and easier, and she had her inheritance coming to her. There were so many bittersweet things associated with the money.

Her father had lived like a miser and saved every penny he had. She tried to imagine her mother serving meals like this to her friends.

Cruz came out in the new clothes Isola had bought him. She was glad he didn't make a big deal about the gift. She motioned for him to close the door behind him. He stood proud in his new khaki pants and navy linen shirt. The fit was perfect. He did several turns for her, just as she had done for him when showing off the red dress she had brought from San Francisco. She laughed at his twirls.

"I don't know whose these are, but they fit. No?"

"Well, they're not mine." She admired her selections. She used to buy Jeremy clothes all the time. Although men's clothes were so much easier to size than women's, she had taken the liberty of checking his clothes. She was proud of herself.

She remembered the Polaroid camera she had found in the closet. She ran upstairs, then took several snapshots of Cruz in front of the sofa, then Cruz doing a Hollywood pose, then one of her and Cruz with only their eyes filling the frame. He grabbed the camera and started snapping shots of her. They ran out of film and Cruz changed into his old clothes.

Isola rolled him a taco. He pulled her close and puckered his lips. She pacified him with a taco instead. He swiveled the taco up and down the way a baby would.

"You have your mother's pout." He wolfed down the rest of the taco and grabbed a napkin.

"What do you mean?" She pushed her plate aside.

"Mmm. This is good. What's in this?" Cruz helped himself to more rice.

"No. What do you mean about my mother's pout?" Isola leaned in closer to him and exaggerated her scrunched up lips and frown.

"I didn't know her very well, but I saw her make the face you just made. That's all."

"Are you going to work soon?"

"In the morning. I found work at Thornton, the furniture factory I told you about."

"Can I give you a ride tomorrow so you won't have to take the bus?"

"No es necesario."

"I know, but I want to see where you'll be working."

Cruz didn't answer.

"Your food is cold."

"If it will make you happy, you can give me a ride, but only this one time, OK?"

The next morning she drove him to the Thornton Furniture factory. It wasn't far, but Isola knew she had saved Cruz from a long wait for the bus. His hand waving good-bye reminded her to call him back toward the car. She flagged him over and he approached her open window.

"What time can I pick you up?"

"I don't think I'll need a ride. I might work a second job."

"But you know you don't have to. You can stay with me. I might have more work or I can give you some money."

"That's why I didn't want you to drive me. I need to work. I need to send money to my parents. I don't want you to give me everything."

A sense of admiration for this hard-working man rose in her chest and she blurted out, "You're sweet. I love you," and kissed his hand. He stood frozen, as if she had kicked him out of the house and told him never to come back. Apparently, saying those three words was worse. She hadn't meant to blurt out the L-word, but there it was. She had said it, and at least Renée wasn't around to scold her and tell her she was jumping into things too fast, the way she always did. When it came to boys, she always fell hard and fast. She hoped that Cruz would be different, that he would be happy to hear her declaration of love. But Cruz didn't seem to make much out of her declarations. She was beginning to understand that he needed to roam free and didn't want to play house with her. She held her breath, then managed to breathe. She had acted this role before. The words to the script seemed to fly out of her mouth in well rehearsed phrases.

"Will I see you tomorrow?" She continued to star in her drama.

"Of course."

She didn't believe him. She didn't believe herself. She didn't care that things were happening fast. "Of course" was not an acceptable answer for a man with few or no cares in the world and a woman who was in too deep. She wished she could send her words back where they had come from. Why didn't she say something the other night in bed, instead of making Cruz feel like a smothered schoolboy and blurting her feelings from a car window? She was the Awkward Moment Queen. At that moment, she crowned herself the reigning champ of awkward moments.

When Isola returned to the house she found a car blocking the garage. She honked and the car slowly moved forward. Josefina stepped out of the car and walked toward her. Isola had had a premonition she'd see Josefina again. And, here she was, wearing a brown dress, a uniform from a hotel or a restaurant.

"Disculpa. I want to speak to you before I go to work."

"Pásale." Isola opened the door for her. "¿Café?" She poured her some coffee. "I see that you're on your way to work. I don't have those papers for you. I'm sorry."

"I know your mother left them for me. I can help you look for them." She set her coffee on the table.

"It's not that I need help looking. Well, I have needed some help, but I have a friend helping me." Isola didn't know what she wanted to say. She blurted out the words without thinking first while pacing the room.

"I didn't know you had friends here. Who is your friend?" Josefina raised her eyebrows and gave a strange and suspicious look. Her voice sounded both mocking and scolding.

"You've already mentioned that I don't have friends here and you've already met Cruz. I'm sorry, but I don't have anything for you. I honestly haven't found those papers."

"Cruz. Yes. I know all about Cruz. You don't know what you've done. Your mother wouldn't want you to give him anything. He deceived her the way he's deceiving you. Don't you know?"

"Enough!" Isola raised her hand. "I need to ask you to leave."

"You're going to regret taking up with Cruz."

"You come here to judge me and ask me over and over again for the same impossible papers. Don't come here anymore." Isola slammed the door behind Josefina.

Almost three days had passed and Isola hadn't heard from Cruz. She thought she had made a really big mistake in blurting out her feelings for him. It was true they had no ground rules. They weren't married and it was too soon to broach the subject. She didn't know why she expected more from him, but she did. The last time he disappeared for two days, now it was three. Don't beat yourself up. At least you were smart enough to see where he was working. Give yourself a little credit.

She didn't have an address for Thornton, but she'd find the place. She had paid close attention to the route as Cruz grunted to turn here and there, but it had been in pre-dawn darkness and she had managed to get lost on the way home from the factory. She found the address in the phone book and written it down in case she got lost. Twenty minutes was all it took to pull into the factory's lot.

The smell of sawdust and oak inside the factory tickled her nose. She didn't see any women working there and she could feel the men stealing glances at her. A phone call would've sufficed, but she always had to do things the hard way. She stopped a man who was speaking Spanish into a walkie-talkie.

"¿Conoces a Cruz?"

"¿Cruz quién? Pregúntale al jefe, Mr. Davis. Espere aquí." The man's shirt said "Rick" in blue cursive letters.

Isola had a feeling she wouldn't find Cruz. Earlier she had fantasized about taking him to lunch, about his harrowing tale of what had happened to him and his telling her that he couldn't wait to finish his shift to see her.

"¿Dónde está el jefe? Dígale que lo busca una muchacha," Rick yelled to the men moving a tabletop.

"Cinco minutos," another man yelled back.

Isola waited in his office. She surveyed Mr. Davis's mementos and picked up a photograph of a woman seated in a rocking chair, cradling a small baby. Isola jumped and almost dropped the picture when she turned to find a man blocking the doorway, watching her.

"That's my wife." He reached for the photograph and looked at it eagerly as though he hadn't seen it in years.

Isola could tell he wanted her hands off his photos. "She's beautiful. How many kids do you have?"

"Just our daughter, Emily." Mr. Davis rubbed dust off the picture with his sleeve.

"You're looking for me?"

"You must be Mr. Davis."

"Are you with the INS or worker's comp?"

"It's nothing like that." Isola lowered her head.

"Let me guess. One of these guys is your lover."

"No. I'm trying to help a friend." Isola pulled out the Polaroid she had taken of Cruz. "I'm looking for this man. His name is Cruz Zárate."

Mr. Davis sat at his desk, lit a cigarette, and leaned back while he inhaled. "Cruz. These guys are always changing their names. Are you sure it's Cruz?" Mr. Davis reached for the bifocals in his shirt pocket and inspected the Polaroid. He looked at the photo as if the man in the picture owed him something. "Cruz. I remember the face. Why are you looking for him?"

"He's a friend. When was the last time you saw him?" Isola coughed. She felt a choking sensation from the cigarette smoke and her eyes started to water.

"About four days ago." Davis sat down at his desk and pulled out a ledger book. "He's scheduled to work next week."

"Why next week?"

"I don't know. That's what he signed up for. I'm pretty flexible here. Most of these guys juggle several jobs. I can see you're worried." He took another drag from his cigarette. This time he took care not to blow the smoke in her face as he spoke. "But I don't get why you care about a guy like him. Does he owe you money?" He gave her the kind of smirk Jeremy used to flash her when he thought he knew better.

"Nothing like that," Isola said. "Not that it's any of your business." Who was this guy? His wood-paneled-sawdust-strewn office didn't make him some hotshot.

"Maybe. But you're not the only woman to come in here and try to help out one of these guys. Take a look around. Any one of these guys could be your Cruz. Do you think they'd give a shit about you? Hell, they don't care who helps them. They'll take you for all you've got."

She didn't care to hear more and walked away as he yelled his last sentence.

21

Take a Little Trip

His first time in a flashy car named *Bomba Verde*. Cruz didn't understand what the big deal was. Nacho pressed hard on the accelerator and the car barely moved. Chandler Boulevard looked different from inside *Bomba Verde*. The car jerked like a whipped mule being forced to trot. Cruz had never seen Nacho more excited. Lifting one wheel, then dropping the car to lift the next, until Nacho slammed *Bomba Verde* hard against its frame. The tricked-up car sure could bounce. Cruz grabbed his sides. His kidneys vibrated with the muffler's grinding suspension. The car belonged to Nacho's cousin from California and Cruz wondered if all people from California wanted to be famous movie stars.

"You passed the store," Cruz said.

"Let's ride, man. My cousin's Chevy is bad, ain't it?" Nacho pressed a button under the steering wheel that made the car bounce up and down. He rolled down the window and called out to a woman waiting for a bus under the shade of the only tree on the block. Cruz turned on the radio and ran his hand across the polished black dashboard. They drove almost to the Indian reservation, until Chandler Boulevard became more sparse and dusty like the streets on the outskirts of Atlixco. Nacho switched the radio to KZAG, Arizona oldies. He didn't know the words, but it didn't matter. By the middle of the song, even Cruz knew when to yell out "I'm your puppet" to the song's lazy rhythm.

"Is it true your cousin drove this car all the way from EasLos to show Trini?" Cruz reached down for the lever and stretched his seat back.

"No way. He wanted to impress Pifi's friend Lene."

"Do I know Lene? Is she the one with a little kid and two older ones?" Cruz thought of the young woman's empanada-shaped rear and the way she moved like a pregnant duck, swaying heavily, almost worse than doña Trinidad.

"Yeah, she was something else before Gabriel went to California. Even after having five kids, she's foxy."

"Mira." Cruz called Nacho's attention to the police car parked between two rows of cactuses. He turned his face down to avoid the policeman's eyes.

"So what? I seen him a mile away. He ain't gonna do nothing." Nacho passed the parked car and looked straight at the officer.

"They're waiting for us and we passed the store." He stared in front of him. Cruz combed a strand of hair back with his fingers. He noticed the setting sun behind him. Mango colors lit the horizon.

"Who's waiting for us? The cops only keep cars in México. We're not doing anything wrong. But we'll go back because you're a pussy." Nacho spun the car around and came to a screeching halt at the stoplight. He missed crashing into a pickup truck by seconds.

"Ay, he's going to think you're drunk."

"Drunk! I only had one beer. It's your fault for all your crying and ruining our good time." He slowed down and drove toward the setting sun.

Flashes of blue and red stroked the car's mirror. Cruz's heart pounded and he tried to speak. He wanted to say, "I told you so, cabrón," but the words wouldn't come out. By the time Cruz caught his breath, Nacho started to panic and the cop car closed in on them.

"Now what do we do?" Cruz looked at Nacho as if he had traded his soul and life for two pennies.

"Don't look like that," Nacho said. "Remember when we pretended we were cleaning the floors at Tosca?" Cruz nodded. That was over two years ago, maybe longer. He vaguely remembered the one time he and Nacho stayed at the empty building. "The cops came in to disturb our sleep; that's all. They asked us a few questions and left us alone. They just want to mess with us and make sure we're not drunk. Don't worry. They won't do anything."

Easy for him to say "don't worry," Cruz thought. Nacho had papers and a job. Noise blared from the squad car's bullhorn. Cruz didn't understand the garbled words, but he knew he'd better pray for a miracle. Nacho pulled into the Food City parking lot without hesitation. Cruz sank into the car's leather seat. What would they do to him? Send him back, probably. A second police car parked in front of the green Chevy. They were blocked in. Nacho squeezed his gold cross, kissed it, and hid the chain under his shirt. They sat still. The policeman approached and Nacho rolled down his window. The policeman smiled and greeted them. Cruz was relieved when the police officer's Spanish words sounded familiar and friendly. But he didn't like the way the policeman kept his hand over his gun.

"We're going to avoid a big scene," the policeman said. He asked Nacho questions about the car and why he had made an illegal U-turn. Nacho said he hadn't seen the no U-turn sign. The policeman sifted through the car's registration papers and listened to Nacho's explanation about the car and his cousin who was visiting from California.

"Not bad," he said. "I've had a joyride or two in a car like this." The officer leaned heavily on the door.

"Can we go?" Nacho said.

"Calma. Not so fast. Put the keys on the dashboard where I can see them." He tore the top sheet off the thick ticket. "I have to do some extra work with the FEDS and INS this week. We need to see your friend's ID." He pointed to the man seated in the squad car facing them. The man in the black T-shirt with large white letters that spelled "FED" smiled and waved.

"I showed you my driver's license."

"I said I need your friend's papers too."

"But he didn't even bring his wallet. It was still at the house when we took the car for a ride," Nacho said.

"Can't he talk? Is he visiting too?" The officer's smile disappeared as he addressed Cruz. "Where do you live?"

"Three six three nine Los Feliz." Cruz carefully pronounced each number in English. He knew he sounded dumb like a drunk gringo.

"What city and state do you live in?" The officer scribbled on a small notepad.

Cruz tried to shape his mouth in the same way Isola formed her words when she spoke on the telephone or blurted out things in English to him. But his "Chandler" sounded like "chandelier" and his "California" chopped up too many syllables as his tongue uselessly rolled his "r."

"What kind of identification do you have?" He asked his question and continued to take notes without looking up at Cruz.

"I have California I.D."

"Do you have it with you?"

"Yes."

"Name and date of birth?"

"Marcel Palan, 1969," Cruz said.

Both the policeman and Nacho looked at Cruz with doubt.

"Step out of the car." The officer frisked Cruz and pulled a leather wallet from his back pocket and opened it. He stared at the card for a long time.

"Get back in the car. Keep your hands where I can see them." He motioned for Cruz to place his hands on the dashboard. The officer walked back to his car.

"Hijo de tu madre. Who's Marcel Pa— ¿Qué dijistes?"

"Palan. Remember?" Cruz said.

"Oh, yeah. So, it went all right . . ." Nacho stopped talking when he saw the police approaching again. "No digas nada más," he said quickly.

"You both need to answer more questions at the station."

The officer stuffed the wallet in his pocket, tightened handcuffs around Cruz's wrists, and shoved him toward the squad car. He said something about needing to check the car's registration at the station. Nacho had assured Cruz there wouldn't be any problems with borrowing his cousin's car. Cruz didn't expect the policeman to take Nacho as well. Neither of them had done anything wrong, and Nacho had always, until now, had good luck with cops.

22

One Allowed

A pretty police lady spoke to him in Spanish mixed with English and then in English mixed with Spanish. Cruz didn't understand everything, but he knew he could leave as soon as he called someone for a ride. He and Nacho had been taken to the station for more questioning, but there were no charges. Nacho had warned him not to call Pifi or Trini or anyone they knew. Nacho didn't want his aunt to start panicking and asking favors from their friend, officer Ed Ortega. The sorry look on Nacho's face worsened when Cruz told Nacho he had used his phone priviledge to call Isola.

The police lady eyed him while he dialed the number and waited. It rang five times before he heard Isola's voice.

"Isola." Cruz didn't know what to say.

"I've been worried. You disappear and don't call for days. Where are you?"

Her voice was so loud, Cruz pulled the phone away from his ear.

"En la cárcel. I need a ride."

"What happened? Speak up! I can barely hear you. What did you do? Why are you in jail?"

"Pa' nada. I was riding in a car with my friend, Nacho, that's all we were doing. They say they are dropping the charges. But I don't know what the charges were. Something about an illegal U, but there was no sign." The lump in his throat cleared and he could speak more clearly.

"Tell me exactly what happened."

"My friend wanted to show me his cousin's car. I didn't want to go. We barely rode three blocks before we both were arrested."

"Typical," Isola said. "I'm calling my lawyer. I'm sure you didn't do anything to warrant this arrest. Mom always complained that Mexicans were treated unfairly by the police." Her voice grew louder.

"Wait. Don't call a lawyer. They're letting us go. We only need a ride."

"It will be better if you talk to a lawyer."

"Please, no lawyers. Just meet us in front of the jail. I'm calling more for my friend Nacho, Jesús Romero. He has a job that he needs to get to."

"That's nice you're concerned about your friend, but you have places you need to be too."

"I have to go now. Can you come for us?"

"Yes, of course. Don't worry. I'm glad you called. I won't call my lawyer."

"Gracias," Cruz said.

"Let me talk to someone. I need to know where you are."

Cruz was impressed at how easily Isola took charge of things. He didn't really understand the charges or what was going on. At least the police lady was nicer than the cop who arrested him. She gave Isola all kinds of street names and numbers and directions. Isola. Her name made him think of her laughter. If she found him, she'd take him back to her clean house. Doña Marina's house. He wished his bail was already posted or that he could wait for Isola in the office instead of being packed like sardines in the holding room.

The faces in the small cell resembled Cruz's own dark features. He thought the men could've all been from Atlixco. A young vato with a white undershirt and "Madre" tattooed in cursive letters beneath a rose nodded to them. He seemed normal, but the rest of the guys had crooked faces, eyes too wide with susto, as though they had seen evil incarnate. One of the men, a skinny gringo, wasn't mean at all. He had a big closed-mouth smile on his face. Cruz knew he was crazy, maybe crazy enough to kill all of them with his bare hands if they added another person to the crowded room. The skinny gringo's angelic face reminded him of the beggar at the 7-Eleven across from la barda. Cruz tried hard not to stare at the crazy man's face. He didn't mind having to stand so long because sitting on the floor was not going to be possible with the urine and other questionable stains. What he did mind was having to share the same air with all those guys. One of them, probably the skinny gringo, had peed his pants. The stench of urine and farts disgusted him. Cruz was grateful Nacho was with him, even though he was responsible for them being in the can. Nacho had reassured him that police wouldn't arrest them. He was usually right about most things. Nacho had helped him find the place to fix his mica, but he had also gotten him in jail. Cruz didn't care that they were going to drop the charges. Lately he felt that he could no longer trust Nacho. Nacho had been acting so important ever since he got that job chopping lettuce at the taquería. He thought he was better because he wasn't "illegal," even though they had crossed the same muddy river and the same desert. Nacho stood by himself, closer to the scary chueco guys and the young vato. He acted as if he didn't know Cruz. Nacho kept his back to him as if he were the cause of all the bad smells. Finally, Nacho turned toward him. He looked as if he wanted to say something. Cruz only heard him mumble.

"¿Qué cosa? You're the one that wanted to go ride and made me go to your aunt's barbeque," Cruz said.

"I don't want to talk about it. And it's not about the ride or the car."

"Because you think you're too good to be here?"

"¡Pendejo! It's not about me." Nacho raised his voice.

"Then what? That I called Isola for a ride?"

"A ride and what else? I didn't know you were taking up with the daughter, too." Nacho whispered. "And I told you not to call anybody."

"What do you care?" Nacho was starting to piss him off.

"I thought you were tight with my sister." Nacho spoke between clenched teeth.

"You know how it is with Pifi." Cruz had no idea what Nacho was getting at.

"No, I don't know. Why don't you explain it to me," Nacho said. He seemed ready to fight.

"Explain?" Cruz said. He took a step back.

"You know what I think?" Nacho closed in on Cruz. "She's ruined and unwed. If it were anyone else, you'd be a dead man, cabrón."

"She's not!"

"She is."

"I'm not the father." Cruz felt his head throb. He imagined himself being flattened by a train and ascending into heaven, where there were no problems with women or their brothers.

"You are, and you're gonna take care of it. She wanted to tell you herself, but I didn't know about you and Eee-soh-la."

Cruz remembered the last night he had spent with Epifanía. It was before Isola. She had tagged along with him and Nacho to the cantina. Every other time, she always had an excuse, since she always worked on nights they didn't. It was a warm night. Nacho was drunk, and he let Cruz take his sister home. Cruz knew he was lucky. Although she was grown and took care of herself, Nacho never entrusted his baby sister to anybody. The excitement was too much for him. Their lovemaking, although somewhat successful, was over before he could sing her a mañanita. He should've known something was up when Trini gave him a big hug and offered to let him lie down on her bed. At the time, he thought she was joking. She had a way of looking serious when she was making fun of him. It was now obvious he was the only estúpido who didn't know Pifi was pregnant.

"But . . ." Cruz put his hand on Nacho's shoulder.

Nacho jerked him away and moved to the other side of the room. Two of the big guys belted out a long whistle at them as though they were having a lover's fight.

"Leave him alone, niña." The guy with the crooked lip blew a kiss at Cruz.

"You're the maricón and if you don't shut up my homeboys will mess you up." The vato nodded to Nacho and Cruz.

A big guy in a black shirt took a step toward the young vato. "You need your little beaner-homeboys to defend your prissy asses. If I weren't on probation, I'd take care of you so good you wouldn't be able to talk again."

The crazy, angelic gringo spoke up. "Yo, shit-for-brains, blow it out the other end."

Cruz's head felt heavy, as though all of his brain cells had expanded and were about to explode. Nacho was mad at him, the prisoners were going to start a fight, Isola was on her way to pick him up, and Pifi was having his baby. Puta vida. If only Cruz could forget about Nacho and Pifi and the baby. He didn't know how much time had passed. Several hours, it seemed. They added a drunk to the cell. The drunk man smelled like guacamole, tequila, and vomit. He crawled into a ball near the corner and fell asleep. The man smelled worse than the cell. Finally, the police lady came in to let him and

Nacho go. The men started whistling again as they left. The stinky pelado in the corner kept snoring.

Outside the jail, Nacho shook hands and embraced his cousin Ray. Cruz was stunned. He didn't know Nacho had called anybody. He started to ask why he hadn't mentioned talking to Ray when Isola walked up the steps. Cruz recovered from his shock, only to be doubled over by the way Ray was eyeing her. The turquoise dress showed off her tanned skin and pretty legs. She was so beautiful. Ray kept walking past Isola. He said something about getting the car. Nacho started to follow, but decided to wait on the steps. Isola ran toward him. "I'm glad I found you," she said. "The clerk said your friend, Jesús Romero, had been released, but they didn't have a record for you. I was worried they had transfered you or given me the wrong address or something." She spoke quickly and seemed concerned and happy at the same time.

Nacho was right. Cruz was stupid to have called Isola. She didn't know he was using her father's mica and only Nacho knew he had altered her father's papers. If she ever found out, he would be in big trouble with her and the law. Cruz pulled away from her sweet but smothering embrace. She smelled like gardenias.

"Tell me everything that happened. Did you change your mind about the lawyer? What's wrong?" She no longer smiled.

Cruz didn't want to see her face change from happy to scared, but he had to disappoint her and take away her smile. "I can't go with you. I have to stay with my friend Nacho, he's from Atlixco too."

"Is this about that guy in the parking lot? Who is he?"

"Yes. He's Nacho's cousin. I'm sorry to have bothered you. I didn't know that while I was talking with you, Nacho was talking to his cousin. I'm sorry you came all this way."

"You know I don't mind, but what's going on?"

"I need to help them with the car and some other things."

"What other things?"

"Nothing, I'll tell you later."

Nacho motioned to Cruz. It was time to go. Isola waited for Cruz with her hand on hips. Cruz could tell she was getting angry. He walked slowly toward her. Nacho stood up and whispered. "Primero la madre, y luego la hija y tus huevos batidos con mi hermana, buey."

"¡Cállate! Ahí voy." Cruz had had enough of Nacho giving him a hard time, but he didn't like Nacho's stupid little song, "First the mother, and then the daughter, and your balls scrambled with my sister, bull."

Nacho was still mad. Cruz thought he looked madder than when he was in the jail cell. He always complained when Cruz asked to be dropped off at doña Marina's house. Nacho had never approved of either woman.

The three of them eyed one another for what seemed like a long, silent minute. Isola walked toward them. She extended her hand. "Hi, I'm . . ."

Nacho turned his back to her, eyed Cruz one last time before heading for the parking lot.

"Are you coming?" Isola said. "We can go now."

"Ray's waiting," Nacho yelled.

"I'll catch up with you later," Cruz said.

"Ray's waiting," Nacho repeated.

Cruz turned to follow Nacho.

"But aren't you coming with me?"

Cruz spun around again to face Isola. Isola's hand felt cool on Cruz's cheek. He put his hot hand over hers and stroked her hair.

"I have to go with them," he said, "I'll call you later. OK?"

"I came all this way. Is it your friends? Tell them they can trust me."

"It's not that. I'm sorry. I'll explain later. I promise." Cruz ran after Nacho. They got in Ray's car. Cruz turned to see Isola still standing on the steps in front of the jail. She looked sad and dejected, as though she were being abandoned by everyone she knew.

23

Change of Heart

Ray pulled up in front of Trini's house. He seemed in a pleasant mood, but then practically kicked Nacho and Cruz out of the car. "You guys are lucky nothing happened to *Bomba*, ese." Cruz waved to Ray before the darkness of doña Trinidad's house blinded him. All the portable cooling fans were blowing full force and Trini's house was unusually quiet. Epifanía walked up to them and hugged them.

"I'm not even going to ask where the two of you have been."

"You know where we've been," Nacho said.

"Lárgate, Nacho. I have important things to discuss with Cruz." Pifi shoved her brother toward the front room.

"I hope you know what you're doing with this cabrón." Nacho turned toward the living room without looking either Pifi or Cruz in the eye. "Where's my tía?"

"Shopping for the baby." Pifi quickly covered her mouth and stood still, holding her breath.

"He knows," Nacho yelled from the living room.

Pifi stomped her foot, put her hands on her hips, and stuck her tongue out in Nacho's direction.

Cruz stepped closer to her. "Nacho told me."

"Let's go to the back room. I want to show you something."

"The back room?"

"Ven." Pifi led him down the hall to the bedroom across from doña Trinidad's. She tried to cover his eyes, but the hallway was dark and they kept bumping into the wall.

"Mujer, it's so dark in here. I can't see anything."

"But it's a surprise. Oops." They bumped into the wall. "Tía Trini is so excited about being a grandmother that . . ."

"But she's not the grandmother."

"Shst. Don't tell her that." Pifi lightly brushed Cruz's mouth with her hand. "Don't you want to see the room and the things I have for the baby?" Epifanía sounded as though she wanted to cry.

"I'm going to marry you and support the baby, but don't start acting like you're in a telenovela. You're twenty-two and going to be a mother."

"Don't tell me what to do. Who says I need you? I'm not begging you. My tía is so excited about the baby, she's giving us the back room and is shopping for more things right now." Epifanía started to cry for real.

"Cálmate, hija. I'm not telling you what to do."

"Adele's only going to have me clean her house and not send me out on so many other jobs. She even offered to give me a raise." Pifi unloaded her plan between gurgled sobs.

"OK, OK. Don't get upset." Cruz handed her a tissue from a box that was covered in one of Trini's baby blue crocheted masterpieces. "But what does your fruncido cousin say about giving up his room?"

"Don't call my cousin a fruncido. He got that scar on his face defending his mother's good name."

"I'm sorry." Cruz bowed gallantly and swept the ground with an invisible sombrero.

Epifanía swatted his hands. Her doughy belly was exposed and Cruz noticed how much weight she had gained.

"Ós-car," Epifanía said slowly, "is going to live with another relative in Whittier, California, where there's more room for his dogs. Ray's taking him. My aunt, I mean la abuelita, didn't want the pit bulls near the baby. And with Nacho getting in at the taquería and having his own place, it all works out." Pifi smiled as though she had thought of the big plan all on her own.

Cruz saw her smug smile and figured she had come up with her own plan to take him away from Rosalina and Isola and any bit of freedom he might have had.

"I'm sure you had it all figured out."

"Yes, I did." Epifanía sounded proud of herself.

Cruz collapsed on the bed. He didn't feel the same way about Pifi's baby as he did about Rosalina's kids. He had often wished his brother's kids were his own, his brother's bride his own. Marina and then Isola had made him forget about Rosalina. Epifanía only reminded him of everything he had left behind in Atlixco. He didn't want to be a father, but he had no choice. He had been blind to Pifi's condition for the past three months. Epifanía seemed so calm about being pregnant and becoming a mother. Everything came easily to her. Crossing the border any time she wanted, getting good jobs, learning English. Cruz found it hard to endure her excitement. He sat up and looked Epifanía in the eye. "What about that gringo boyfriend you used to hang on?"

"What gringo boyfriend?"

"Don't pretend you don't remember the blue-eyed tijuanero with the long blond hair that competed for jobs at la barda with the mejicanos."

"Vicente? What about him?"

"Well, are you sure it's not his baby?"

"¡Cabrón! It's been over six months since I heard from him and longer than that since we went out. What are you calling me?"

"Nothing. I need to make sure, that's all." He was going to pay for the one time he had taken advantage of Nacho's sister.

"You can ask Trini. She never liked him and didn't want me seeing him. That was all over a year ago."

"Trini never liked me, either!"

"That's not true. You're one of us, from Atlixco. She's a proud abuelita."

"So now it's *abuelita*?" Cruz spread out on the pink-and-white crocheted blanket, another one of Trinidad's handiworks.

As soon as he said the word *abuelita*, Trinidad burst into the room.

"Did I hear someone say my name?"

Cruz was used to Trinidad's disregard for privacy. She had surprised him in the shower once. Trinidad pinched each of Cruz's and Epifanía's cheeks and kissed them both with her breath that always smelled of old bubblegum.

"Wait right here." Doña Trinidad laid a thick hand on each of their shoulders, keeping them prisoner. "You will see Óscar has no hard feelings. He drove me to la Babies-R-Us y mira, look what we bought. ¡Óscar! Trae esa bolsa." Her voice boomed down the hall. Cruz and Pifi covered their ears. "I'm sorry, mija, I didn't mean to scream in your face. Pero mira." She untangled the first item. Pink elephants chased a mouse at the center of the mobile. Trinidad pulled out diapers and bibs and plush toys. Pifi cooed at each pink and blue baby bauble.

Cruz leaned back and let his head flop onto a mound of fluffy pillows. His mind drifted to the days when he was at Marina's house. Her house was often crowded with people. Unlike Trini, Marina took in every beggar that came scratching at her door. But she was good at moving people and helping them get what they needed. Cruz noticed she seemed even better at getting people out of her house after he started sharing her bed. As long as he and Marina had privacy, Cruz didn't care who had walked through her door. Marina was a woman of unparalled passion and experience. She wasn't afraid to take the lead in their lovemaking or tell him what she needed him to do for her. Her hands were always warm, almost fiery. He hadn't met anyone who incited such passion in him since Rosalina. Even Isola wasn't as passionate as her mother. She was more forthright than childlike Epifanía, but sweet and shy with her intimacy. He retreated further into the memories of other women until something soft touching his face made him open his eyes. Pifi was dangling a pink cloth rabbit in front of his face. Cruz wanted out.

"Señora, can I use your shower and a towel?" Cruz asked shyly.

"Mijo, this is your house. You don't have to ask. Mira, I put towels in this dresser for both of you."

How he wished he could run back to Isola's, where he didn't have to ask for towels or anything. He feigned a smile and kissed Trinidad on the cheek. He was used to begging her for things.

"Fúchila." Trinidad fanned the air and pinched her nose. Pifi laughed and seemed delighted by her new family. Cruz wanted to change clothes and wake up from his current nightmare a cleansed man.

24

A Grain of Salt

Isola felt stupid for having driven downtown to bail Cruz out only to have him leave with some guys. She headed toward the freeway, but didn't want to go back to the house just yet. She was tired of sifting through boxes of her mother's things, fed up with her mother's friends, and resentful that her mother's death was taking over her life. Now Cruz had abandoned her. Damn it. It had to be the sex, she told herself. She had allowed herself to fall too deeply for him too fast. Whenever she saw Cruz, she wanted more of him. Through the thick fog of her addiction to him, she knew something was wrong, that he held back more than he gave. The minute she overstepped some random, sensitive boundary, Cruz backed off.

The last time she had seen him, they had made love three times. Cruz made love to her with a passion she had never experienced in a man before. He made love as if he thought it would be the last time he'd ever see her. She relished his intensity and vigor. Her face felt hot from thinking about his stamina. She had a hard time believing a whole week had gone by without her seeing him. Their brief meeting at the jail was bizarre: another perfectly executed awkward moment for the Awkward Moment Queen. She wondered if Cruz had put on some big macho show for his friends. She was too confused to care.

She drove home the long way and exited the freeway at Papago Park, one of the few open spaces in the overpopulated city. The park reminded her that she was in a desert near vast stretches of Saguaro cacti, just as she'd seen in magazines. Isola was beginning to understand the desert. She had quickly acclimated to the heat, but today she was grateful for the unusually cool weather.

The sun started its slow descent and show of fire shadows over the red rocks. A glimpse of the vermillion splash on display over the Phoenix valley made her forget about all of the problems she had inherited. She even imagined herself bringing Jeremy to this spot. Not because she still loved him, but because she'd bet money that seeing the display of sunlight unfiltered by San Francisco fog would cure Jeremy of his self-centeredness and all his other problems. But why bother with Jeremy? She wanted Cruz.

She resolved to kidnap him, make him play hooky from the world. Together they worked. Except for the jail incident, he was a gentleman. She was comfortable talking to him. He was the only person she had taken an interest in since Jeremy. She thought about all the little things he had done for her, and in such a short time, too. The jasmine he had planted in the front yard made the front entrance and garage smell sweet. Their easy lovemaking was simple, and the dry desert air with a hint of sagebrush was Cruz's smell.

After he witnessed the sunset from her special spot, he'd forget about the machismo that was wired into him. She'd get him out of whatever trouble he was in, hire a new lawyer, and fix everything for both of them. She saw a jackrabbit disappear into a distant hole and knew it was time to go home. Home. Her mother's house in Chandler, Arizona, was her home now. Loud rings from her cell phone pulled her out of the fantasy. She saw she had missed two calls from Josefina. She switched off her phone and drove home in silence. With all her problems coursing through her thoughts, she didn't mind being stuck in the Phoenix rush-hour traffic.

She turned onto her street and noticed the jasmine vine that Cruz had planted. The small white flowers glowed purple against the late-setting sun. She rolled down her window to smell another scent she now associated with him. After he had planted the fragrant vine all over the house, he said flowers reminded him of his mother's house in Atlixco. The air was so hot she could see it ripple in space like a dream. She thought she was dreaming when she saw Cruz standing in front of the jasmine. It wasn't a mirage. He was the last person she expected to see tonight; he was coming outside to meet her. After he left with Nacho and acted completely ungrateful, she was sure he'd disappear for another three weeks before she got a phone call from him. She smiled. Damn, she didn't want to smile. She wanted to be mad at him, but she was happy to see him. Still, seeing him paralyzed her. She sat in her car until the back of her neck became damp from the car's heat. She finally commanded her legs to move. She walked inside. He followed her into the kitchen. She felt his body close behind her.

Instead of looking frightened or ashamed of how he had treated her at the jail, he seemed confident—"grown-up" was the word that came to her mind. "I came to apologize," he said.

"I was hoping you'd come, but you're not going to stay. Are you?" Isola poured two glasses of cold water and offered him one.

"No." He accepted the glass. "You're not going to want me to stay when you hear what happened."

"How many times do I have to ask? Don't you trust me?"

"It's not that."

"Then what? Tell me everything. Wait, I want to take you somewhere." Isola got up to look for her keys, her bag. "Where are my keys?" She talked to herself as she retraced her steps. Whatever Cruz had to say would have a better result for her if she took him to her rock; if she could rewind to her view of the sunset, rewind to the last time she was in bed with Cruz, everything would work itself out. Instead, Cruz pulled her close next to the window seat. He looked determined to talk and relieve himself of everything he had bottled up inside. She desperately wanted to alter Cruz's course, but his face said she had no control over what he was about to do or say. She'd seen that look on Jeremy's face when he had told her about himself and Lauren. She slid her arms around Cruz's waist until her fingers touched. She wanted to be wrong about her intuition and the constriction she felt in her throat, as though someone was about to strangle her. She put her head against his chest and felt his breath on her hair before he spoke any words. She closed her eyes, inhaled his jasmine scent. "Tell me." She scooted back against the wall. "Dime," she repeated. "I want you to tell me everything." She made sure her head was touching the wall. If he was going to tell her bad news, which she was certain he was by the beat-up look on his face, as though he had no reason for living, he'd better get it over with.

"Es Epifanía, la hermana de Nacho. She's pregnant. I have to take responsibility." The words rolled off Cruz's tongue smoothly, as though he had rehearsed them over and over. His face was a blank slate as he spilled his news. He might as well have been a robot talking to her. He no longer seemed confident, nor endearing, nor loving. He reported the words as if they were meaningless to him, or to her.

"Responsibility?" A big word. Isola wondered if it was her imagination or if Cruz's English had improved tremendously in the past few days.

"How long have you two been together?"

"It was just one time."

"I don't care how many times you've had sex. I asked how long you've been with her, known her. Do you love her?"

"Don't ask me that."

"I'm asking. Dime."

"I don't love her, but it makes no difference. I have to marry her." Cruz fumbled in his pockets for the key. "I won't bother you anymore."

"Keep it." Isola looked away to wipe her tears.

Cruz tossed the key on the kitchen table.

The worn key on a gold chain made the sound of loose change falling. The key resembled the one Isola had given to Cruz, but there was no yellow sleeve and it had a small ring that spelled *Amor*. A short gasp escaped her. She was certain the ring had belonged to her mother and the key was not the key Isola had given him. The gold ring puzzled her the most. She remembered how fond of the ring her mother had been. Isola had almost forgotten about how her mother used to stand, hunched over the sink, cleaning the dirt from between the letters. *Amor* was one of the first words she learned how to spell because of her mother's love ring. She had assumed her mother had lost the ring years ago. Then there was the key. When she stopped at Home Depot to have a copy made for him, an older clerk chiseled out a new key with sharp edges. Isola bought a brand new yellow plastic sleeve for the key. This key had lost its shine. It looked as though Cruz had been wearing it close to his heart longer than he had known her. She felt drugged and claustrophobic, as though the key had locked her in a different dimension. She steadied herself before speaking. "Not mine," she whispered and looked down at her shoes.

"¿Qué pasa?" Cruz said, "I didn't hear you."

"I said that's not my key." Isola had trouble finding her voice.

"¿Qué?" Cruz put his hand to his ear.

"Don't pretend you don't hear me. This." Isola dangled the key in front of him. She spoke loudly now. "Is not the key I gave you. Are you going to tell me where you got this? Do you have more of these? Did you steal this ring?"

"No." Cruz seemed bewildered. Isola found that the expression on Cruz's face explained everything. He didn't need to say more for her to figure out why he had her mother's ring.

"Don't give me that stupid look. This isn't the key I gave you. Did you take this ring from my mother?"

Cruz blushed and smiled. "It was a gift." He started to talk, then stopped. He took a step toward Isola, then retreated to the opposite corner. He smiled and sighed.

Isola didn't understand his bashful smile or why he acted as if the extra key wasn't a big deal. This was too much to deal with in one day.

"Marina gave me the key and the ring," he said. "I didn't tell you; I didn't tell Nacho or anyone. I almost forgot about the key and it was easy to confuse it with the one you gave me."

"One has yellow plastic and the other a chain and a gold ring. You're telling me you're confused?"

"But . . ."

"No. You didn't tell me because you didn't tell Nacho?"

"Por favor, no es así."

"Don't pretend we're having a communication problem. I think I know what I'm hearing. What about that chain?" Isola pointed to the gold chain Cruz wore around his neck.

"It's just a chain. I am not explaining right."

"What's there to explain? Am I another one of your one-time mistakes too? This is my life. This is my mother we're talking about." Her words sounded loud in her head, but she didn't think she was yelling. She got up only to collapse into a chair at the kitchen table. She was more mad at herself than at him for not having noticed his two sets of keys. In all the times she had slipped money in his pockets, she hadn't noticed he had a key chain with her mother's ring on it. She knew it was no casual gift. There was only one explanation. He had used her mother in the same way he was using her. Her mother had doled out a lot of charity, but she never would have given away her jewelry casually.

"Isola, por favor." He moved in front of her.

"No." She pushed him away but didn't raise her head from the table. "I can't talk now. Come back for your things later." Her body felt heavy, foreign to herself. She refused to look at Cruz. Her head throbbed and she allowed herself to feel wave after wave of a headache course through the space between her eyes and the back of her head.

"But you said I can trust you?" Cruz scrunched his nose and cocked his head in front of her face.

"You come here to tell me about you and this Epifanía woman, but never say anything about you and my own mother?"

"It's not the same."

"Not the same! And you want me to trust you? Do you know what that means? Leave." She raised her head, stood tall, and pointed toward the front door.

The door slammed behind Cruz. He was gone before she finished yelling at him.

She grabbed a Coke from the fridge and took a long sip. She almost finished the can, then burped, a loud, ugly burst of frustration. Her stomach felt more comfortable, but she was unsure about who she was and what she was doing in her mother's house. Then there was Cruz, who had played her all along. He was so familiar with the house. He knew where the gardening tools were and whenever she couldn't find a platter or an iron, he picked out the exact object her mother would've handed her. There were also all the little details he instinctively knew about her. Shortcuts to her psyche that only a mother could know. Either he was taking really good notes whenever she said something or he'd spent an awful lot of time with her mother, who couldn't stop complaining about her. The latter made more sense. Marina never felt the need to call her because she was too busy living a life with Cruz.

She ran upstairs, where she had reorganized her mother's boxes for the second or third time. There was one thing she had to check. She took out the envelope with the "C" on it. When she had first seen the photograph of Cruz, she merely glanced at it and didn't pay much attention. She had noticed the gold chain Cruz wore around his neck. She didn't think much about it, even though it was the kind of necklace a woman would wear. She didn't recognize the necklace as being one of her mother's, but now believed Cruz wasn't beyond wearing the love token. Even if Cruz was telling the truth about already owning the necklace, there was only one explanation of how he came to possess the key and the ring.

What really bothered her was that the envelope wasn't where she had left it, behind Josefina's in the front banker's box, and everything in the box was out of order again. She had taken the time to arrange her mother's boxes and files. There was only one possible explanation. Cruz. He had seen her organize the box and agonize over not finding her father's file countless times and pretended not to have known anything about it. She sifted through the files and took them all out of the box. There were a few stray photographs stuck together at the bottom. Two were the ones Josefina had given her. The other was the missing part of the photograph showing her more clues about her mother's relationships. Now that she had the remaining half in front of her, she could see that the person torn out of the image was a woman. The right arm hugging the man's shoulders was that of her mother. The shape of her arm and the gaudy turquoise and silver ring she always wore on her pinky finger and the *Amor* ring could belong to no one else. All along she had thought that Josefina and her nephew were a threat when she herself was sleeping with her mother's lover. You idiot, she cursed herself. She had let him off too easily. She wanted more answers to questions like where the other half of the torn photograph was. She slid into her mother's gardening shoes and ran down the street after Cruz.

II

The
Sweep

25

The Sweep:
Day One

Bill Davis swung his boots off his desk. He flipped the pages of his calendar and saw that he was not mistaken. Apple One had promised to send him a new guy for the foreman position, but nobody had shown up in three days. He relied on the temp agency, especially during the late summer months when his workers took an unsanctioned "familia leave of absence." He had a few weeks to secure one solid foreman to run things for him when he took his own family vacation. His wife wouldn't forgive him this time if he didn't square everything away by the time their daughter arrived from her college break. Thinking of his daughter reminded him of the young woman, Isola, who had come looking for one of the workers. Pretty face with green eyes like a china doll's. He didn't know what she was thinking behind those marbled eyes, but guessed the young lady thought she was going to waltz into his factory and find her boyfriend sanding wood or hauling finished pieces. He was sure she had no idea about the kinds of guys who worked for him. After fifteen years owning Thornton Furniture, only a dozen of his sixty employees had been with him from the start. Mostly Mexican. They worked hard until they got the itch to see their mamas or their wives and kids and take their so-called familia leave. Davis knew half the men had families both here and south of the border. Some of his workers disappeared like suds; most returned after six weeks. Six weeks was the magic number for how long it took the men to take care of their familia business. He spat in a handkerchief and dusted off the photos of his daughter, Emily. He heard a commotion in the back assembly and thought it must be the new guy who had finally arrived, and was receiving a hard time from the bench crew for being late. The saw's piercing wail went silent, then he heard the chifleros; the men's whistles meant the place was crawling with Feds and INS. *Not another raid. Son of a bitch.* He turned to grab his cash drawer.

"Stay right where you are, Davis." Davis didn't have to look up to know Bob What's-His-Face, the troublemaker from the INS, was hovering. Davis had a hard time remembering names, but he never forgot a voice. The patter of boots clunked around the building. Davis noticed there were more men than usual.

"I'm behind with my orders. I'll get what you need so we can be done here." Davis pointed to his safe.

"It's not going down like that. We're working with City Hall, Mesa and Chandler Police. Sheriff's in charge of this one." Bob stood firm in front of the door and called off one of his men with a flick of his wrist.

"Shit. Bob. Why now? Come on." Davis didn't mean to sound so whiny, but he had to make a plea to save his business.

"I'd shut my mouth if I were you. I'd shut down the factory too, for at least another four days." Bob turned to look behind him. He kept his radio held high like a weapon.

"Aw, come on, Bob, what'll it take, 400 dollars?" Davis didn't recognize any of the cops. Usually INS handled the illegal raids and Bob accepted his cash and took the men who weren't pulling their weight. INS bagged their illegals, the temp agency sent him better replacements, Bob made some pocket change for his wife and kids, and the men they deported crawled back and begged for their jobs in six weeks.

"Keep your money. It ain't gonna help." Bob motioned for him to stay in his office. His face seemed sympathetic but firm.

Davis saw Felipe, his assembly line manager being arrested by a baby-faced rookie.

"Hey, he's got papers," Davis shouted, "He's legit." Davis walked slowly toward Felipe and the rookie.

"I asked him three times to show me a green card, ID, whatever he got and all he does is shrug his shoulders, give me a dumb, disrespectful look," the rookie said.

Davis hated how rookies loved their power trip.

"Se me olvidó la cartera con mi lonche. Dígales que tengo papeles. Jefe, la mica está en mi casa." Felipe begged his boss for help.

"If you take him in, you're only going to have to let him go. He has papers. He says he forgot his wallet and his lunch. I can read you his numbers."

"He don't even speak English and you expect me to believe he has papers." The rookie pushed Felipe against the chain link fence and gave Davis a look that said he better keep quiet.

"He's my chief operator, been with me for almost ten years. Give me a break."

"Not my problem you hiring wets."

"He's a legal resident."

"One more peep out of you and I'll arrest you for obstruction of justice."

Felipe, Raúl, the twins, and all eight of the unrelated Garcías were lined up against the fence. Sweat ran down their faces and arms. Davis wanted to give them water, something to calm his men. He knew he was their only hope. But there was nothing he could do. Feds and cops were everywhere, in the cutting room, all over the front floor display, and outside, surrounding the chain-link fence. Davis didn't check the lockers and back storage offices, but he suspected agents were there too. He had never been invaded with so much manpower before. It was the first time the police and the city had worked together in immigration affairs. The Feds were unwilling to negotiate. Their hands hovered over their weapons. After his plea for Felipe, they kept him away from the line of men. Davis knew it wasn't the first time in history big government had gotten anxious about Mexicans working for small businesses like his, panicked, and started their roundups. He knew their little operation wouldn't last more than a week. But it was enough to make him lose more money than he cared to calculate. He'd have to hire a whole new batch of workers and keep the wages from most of the deported men. If Felipe and the twins pulled bail, he'd hire them back in a second and give them a bonus for coming back. No one else, though; he couldn't afford it. Shit.

Davis looked down the street and saw that the rookie didn't even have a squad car. He was on a bicycle. Cops on bicycles, that's a new one, he thought. The cop had called for reinforcements. They filled three white vans with forty of his workers. Davis wondered how the cop on the bicycle was going to round up all of his men.

Bob performed one last slow sweep before ordering the vans and bicycle units to leave. Davis waited until the vans were out of sight and then surveyed the damage. They hadn't taken Lee and Tran, the Vietnamese brothers, nor the three white guys that stuck together like brothers, Spud, Doc, and Jimbo.

"I saw the police arrest 'em all. What they do?" Jimbo's crooked frown showed concern. The men huddled in Davis's office and waited for him speak.

"Cops assisting on a wetback raid, was all. They took everyone who looked Mexican or who didn't speak English. Take the rest of the week off; we'll open up on Monday." He clapped his hands as if that was the best play he could come up with.

"You gonna pay for the whole week?" Jimbo spoke up.

Davis nodded.

"Thanks, boss." Jimbo said solemnly. The others followed in their expressions of thanks and relief.

Davis nodded to the men. "Did anyone get hurt?"

"Not really," Jimbo said. "There was this hairy moment when García Uno was backing up with a futon siding and he didn't see the cop on account of the wood blocking his view. And Joe starts giving him sign language to tell him about the cop. Only García Uno thinks he's telling him his fly's undone, he grabs his crotch and it looks likes he's telling the cop he ain't got balls. If it weren't for the cop's partner who sees the whole thing and helps García Uno with the board, he might've had his balls blown off, ha." Jimbo's laughter fills the factory. Three other men join in and Davis laughs with them.

"Come back Monday."

After the last worker left, Davis counted his cash drawer. The money was all there.

He didn't put it past Bob to hit him extra hard on this joint job with the Feds and cops.

What am I going to tell Abby? His wife had been nagging him for all sorts of shit, shit that required money. He stood to lose a good deal of money. Thanks to Bob and the Feds, he'd have to cancel their vacation with Emily. He had a feeling this year would be the last family trip the three of them would take before their only daughter married. His wife was going to lay into him hard when he broke the news. He went into the break room and scanned the time sheet ledgers to figure out who had shown up today and who was missing. From the open lockers, abandoned shirts, scattered thermoses, and the three crates stacked near the wall, it looked as if some of the workers had tried to escape through the back window. He climbed the stack of crates.

"Yup," he said.

Some of the men had made their escape. But there was no use opening tomorrow since Bob had hinted they were going to play roundup for the rest of the week. Who was going to compensate him for his workers, some of them legal residents? Davis was furious again. Who had sicced the INS on him? He suspected one person, Kennedy Chaplin. Chaplin with his shoddy Ethan Allen knockoffs. He'd give the bastard a piece of his mind. Davis thought for a second, then grabbed the telephone and punched his number.

"Hello," Chaplin said.

Davis didn't recognize his voice. The usual cocky attitude was missing.

"Any idea who paid off the Feds to shut me down?"

"I was wondering the same damn thing."

"You too? Anyone else?"

"I heard from my brother-in-law down south in Yuma, our manufacturers in Chandler, and Wayne at the Danish outfit in Mesa. Cops are having themselves a roundup fiesta," said Chaplin. "When I heard the chifleros start their whistling, I suspected what was going on. But it was too late; Feds rounded up most of my men. Told me to close up shop."

"They told me the same."

"I heard they're even picking up Mexican women and children at bus stops and Laundromats." Chaplin's scratchy laugh turned into a hacking cough.

"Women and children?" Davis wasn't up for taking on the local police and the INS.

He hung up. For once, he didn't have anything more to say to Kennedy Chaplin. They were both suffering.

26

The Sweep:
Day Two

Epifanía thought an earthquake was ending her world. She roused herself and parted the curtains. Nacho pounded on the door as they do in the movies just before the police kick it in. She waved until he saw her. The house stopped shaking at last.

"¿Qué te pasa?" She opened the door to Nacho, who looked terrified. His front teeth bit into his lower lip, as though he was trying not to cry.

"¿Y Óscar? ¿Mi tía Trini? Where are they?" Nacho choked out his hurried words.

"They're at the store. Ay, Nacho. If the baby comes out early it's your fault with all that banging." She rubbed her growing belly.

"Quit being so selfish. I'm trying to help you and Cruz and Óscar. Where's Cruz?" He walked past the dark living room and collapsed into a kitchen chair.

"¿Quién sabe dónde está ese fulano?" Epifanía shrugged her shoulders. Nacho knew more about Cruz's whereabouts than she did. "You know how that rascal has a way of disappearing on us. ¿Qué pasa?"

Nacho lifted his head and waited for Epifanía to sit next to him. "I was on the bus when I saw Pedrito. He told me not to come to the restaurant, not to go to Alberto's apartments. I thought he was messing with me because I took his job and he had to wait a few weeks for Alberto's to hire him back. But the look in his eyes told me he was serious."

"But why didn't he want you to go to work?"

He grabbed Epifanía's arm and shook it. "Because la migra's been busy the past two days. Arresting everybody, even people with clean micas. That's why."

"Shut up! You can't be serious." Epifanía eyed her brother. He wasn't making any sense.

"Yes, they're even taking children off the streets and grandmothers out of their houses."

"¡Nacho, no seas exagerado! You can be such a liar. Don't believe everything you hear."

"For real. That's what I heard. I swear." Nacho raised his right hand and put his left over his heart.

Epifanía clasped her heart and let out a big sigh. "Then you better stay here with us until they stop the raids."

"I'm not afraid of them. I'm not a dog."

"No, hombre, but they'll treat you like a dog with your attitude. Didn't you say they were taking babies and abuelitas?"

"OK, maybe I exaggerated a little. I only wanted to make sure you understood. And to warn Óscar. And Cruz."

"Take your own advice. They've caught you once already."

"But that was completely different. And you know it."

"I get scared when you start acting stubborn." Epifanía picked at the tortilla she had buttered earlier. She lifted it to offer Nacho a bite.

He shook his head. "Don't worry about me," he said. "Stay with Adele. Somewhere outside of Chandler and Mesa. I heard they're patrolling the streets, picking 'Mexicans out like head lice,' that's what those pinches are saying about us."

"Ay, the things you hear. Don't exaggerate with me. I've had enough exaggerated feelings." Epifanía watched Nacho disappear around the corner. She locked the door. She wasn't going anywhere until Óscar and Trini returned. If they take Cruz, pues ni modo, there's nothing to be done, she thought. She didn't think he seemed happy with her and she had grown accustomed to seeing less of him.

27

The Sweep:
Day Three

Only twenty-three minutes had passed since Nacho had left a toda máquina, like a fast locomotive, when the phone rang.

"Diga." Epifanía sat down in Trini's kitchen in the same wobbly chair Nacho had used.

It was Adele. "Pifi, I'm so glad you answered. How are you?"

"Fine." She wanted to ask if she could stay in her old room for a few days, but Adele's voice sounded funny and high-pitched, as if she were going to ask her for a favor.

"My girls are running out on me. Since you've taken your maternity leave early, could you please clean Mr. Schmidt's house this week? You've always liked his generosity and he doesn't require much, more of a formality."

"Nacho told me about the police picking up Mexicans. Don't try to blame me for your missing girls."

"I'm not blaming you, Pifi. I'm asking for your help. I'll pay you generously, a little extra cash for your baby."

"Lo siento, Adele. My feet and back hurt. I like Mr. Schmidt, but I can't go anywhere today." Mr. Schmidt's fat tips were enticing, but Epifanía knew it was safer for her to stay at her tía's. If the police arrested her, they wouldn't care that she was pregnant. In fact, they'd kick her out of the country and ask questions later.

"How about tomorrow or early next week? I would really appreciate it."

Epifanía had never heard Adele whine and beg before. She always gave orders and never used words like "please" and "thank you" and "I appreciate it," but her kind words weren't going to help her this time.

"Only if you bring the car for me. I'm not taking the bus."

"I can do that this one time." Even with all her begging, Adele's commanding tone made it clear she was the boss.

28

The Sweep:
Day Four

Trini licked chocolate from her fingers and set the rest of her Baby Ruth on the night stand. She took off her slippers and adjusted her blanket. *María la del Barrio* was about to start and she didn't want any interruptions. King kept barking. *Óscar is supposed to keep that animal from making noise during my novela!* Trini waddled down the hallway. She opened Epifanía's door. Where did that girl go? She hadn't noticed Epifanía leave the house.

"¡Cállate, King!" Trini slapped her hands together.

The dog barked more furiously. Trini rushed outside. She sensed the dog was trying to tell her something. Too many strange things had happened this week. The corner store was closed and the man who had delivered her Sparkletts water for the past twelve years was missing. The company sent a young kid who wasn't aware of her special arrangement with señor Escamilla, how he delivered her bottled water regardless of whether or not she had the money to pay. She always caught up with her bill within two or three months. And she was furious and frightened after hearing Epifanía tell Nacho's story about how la migra was stealing babies from Laundromats. She didn't believe most of the stories, but anything was possible. Dios mío. What next?

"¡Cállate!" She yelled at the dog again. She slammed the door closed and checked outside the window to see what the dog was barking at. She saw a group of four men and one woman huddled in front of the Rodríguez's house across the street. There was a fifth man who had been hidden behind a policeman whom she also recognized. Her street was busy. She also noticed three policemen on bicycles circling the neighborhood. Officer Ortega led Óscar to the grass. She spotted her nephew's skinny legs and flat nalgas; she didn't know how he kept his jeans on with such a flat butt and narrow hips. When it looked as though Óscar was arguing with Ed Ortega, Trini started out to meet them. But they both waved their arms and motioned for her to stay where she was. She looked down at her clothes. She was decent enough: she had on a dress, a robe, and slippers. It wasn't as if she were coming out in her slip and bra. She had every right to come out, but she waited for the officer on her porch.

Óscar seemed scared. He was nervously rubbing his fingers, as though praying a rosary. The officer motioned to his hands. Óscar stopped fidgeting with his fingers; he lifted his hands and let them rest on his thighs. As the officer approached, she eyed the big ears, long nose, and thick, black hair of Officer Ortega. He had cousins from Atlixco and was like family. What business did he have with Óscar? She tapped her foot and waited for him to speak.

"Doña Trinidad, it's been a long time." Officer Ortega held out his hand.

"We're not going to be friends until you bring Óscar. You know he hasn't done anything." Trini shoved her fists into the pockets of her cotton robe.

"I've talked to him and he's more concerned about you missing your show and about his dog than about being detained." Officer Ortega smiled and waved to Óscar, who gave a slight nod.

"See how kind Óscar is. He's always thinking about others. Why are you detaining him?" Trini repeated the awful word. "De-tain-ing, y por nada. He hasn't had time to do anything."

"I'll tell you how it is. We're working with the INS. We were investigating the house across the street. Unfortunately, Óscar was arguing with the residents of 2713 about his dog. INS got to him first."

"But I'm his sponsor."

He put his hand on her back. "Then it will be a formality. He'll be back after a short period. You know the drill."

She stepped away from his hand patting her back. "You people have done this before. Óscar is hardworking." Officer Ortega tried to step closer to her and calm her, but she wasn't going to let him take Óscar without trying a few tricks of her own. "Mira, why don't you take the woman from the last house on this street? The one with the red rocks in the front yard. She came over here just to have her baby."

"Excuse me for a minute." He turned his back and answered his radio.

Trini tapped officer Ortega on his shoulder, but he no longer seemed to be paying attention. She didn't recognize the kid who'd come around to check on her. He was all business. She lowered her voice to sound more formal. "Ed, listen, allá, over there, in the beige house, those two brothers son malos, they're real mean and there's always pleito on the weekends when they have cockfights in the backyard. You've been there before. Take them or . . ."

"Enough, doña Trinidad. I don't need to hear any more. I'll see what I can do. The vans are coming."

"What vans?" Trini grabbed hold of the iron railing. She felt faint.

"That's all I can tell you. I have to go. I suggest you stay inside or you'll have to deal with the INS."

"I don't care who I have to deal with. I have papers. No soy mojada."

She had lost sight of Óscar. Officer Ortega joined the two others. While she had tried to convince Ed to leave Óscar out of the roundup, the other officers had gathered more of her neighbors, including the pregnant woman she had told Ed about. She felt sick to her stomach for having told on her neighbor, but Óscar was in trouble. Years ago, she had seen la migra round up people. It's all about numbers, she remembered from the last time. The government got scared because they saw too many Mexicanos and then they started with their interrogations, their arrests. She had seen this happen more than once. A white van turned onto her street. Trini clutched her chest. She felt as though her heart was being run over by a truck. The officers loaded the group in the van and took Óscar. Officer Ortega spoke into his radio and nodded to Trini. He hopped on his bicycle and pedaled away. She spat on the ground before locking her doors.

29

The Sweep:
Day Five

Isola knew she'd kick herself if she didn't get some answers now that she'd discovered the truth about Cruz. He couldn't have gotten too far and he'd have to wait at least another fifteen minutes before his bus came. She blamed herself for believing what she had wanted to see, but she still couldn't believe his nerve. Isola caught up with Cruz at the bus stop and was prepared to use her loud teacher voice and raise a scene in the middle of the street, but she was out of breath. He looked up and their eyes locked for a few seconds, but he didn't acknowledge her. He looked through her and past her, as though trying to see the bus beyond her small frame. She finally realized Cruz was looking at something, but it wasn't a bus. She didn't hear the bus's familiar whine and squeal. Isola turned around and saw what Cruz had been eyeing. A parade of police cars and vans—military, perhaps. The line of cars made Cruz turn away and start jogging toward the park. Cruz picked up speed. Isola followed. She ran so fast her sides and shins burned. She finally caught up with him.

"¡La migra!" Cruz yelled.

"No, no. Es la policía. Mira, the cars clearly say 'Chandler Police.'" Isola had never seen him act so skittish. "They're leaving the street. Listen to me. I have to talk you."

"Cruzamos el parque y luego damos la vuelta." Cruz grabbed her arm and insisted on taking the long way.

"Through the park? The house is the other way." Isola stopped to catch her breath. Cruz was too far away to hear her. Something had really shaken him up. His frightened look made her worry about his safety. She ran after him. Cruz was too scared to reason with. She caught up with him again. They circled the block. Apparently, the same convoy had circled around too. They were being followed. They jaywalked to reach the house. The envoy started to slow down. Cruz picked up speed.

"¡Apúrate! Es la migra." Cruz waved and motioned for her to hurry up. He wouldn't wait for her.

"What the hell? Slow down." She was out of breath again. Isola let him run down the street. She'd get there eventually.

As she approached him, she saw three men wearing black T-shirts with "FED" written in bold white letters. She was too winded to run and thought it best to approach slowly. By the time she reached them, Cruz was being asked for his ID. The men, policeman or Feds, motioned for her to join them. The events that followed happened both fast and slowly, as if Isola were trying to wake herself up from a bad dream. She heard the men interrogate Cruz about his ID. Only they weren't calling him "Cruz." The policeman, a large man who spoke Spanish, was addressing him by her father's name, Marcel Palan. Cruz seemed to wear the identity like an old shoe. Isola hadn't seen that card in years. Cruz had somehow altered some of the details on her father's license. He had given his own date of birth instead of her father's. She wasn't sure of her father's weight; that could be the same, but he must've changed the photograph on the I.D. and the expiration date. She felt dizzy. They gave the driver's license back to Cruz and let him go.

In slow motion, her tongue went slack and listless. At the same time, the fury she was feeling caused her entire body to freeze and feel both heavy and loose like Jell-O in a lead mold. In fast motion, Cruz walked away. Isola was still processing the full impact of his betrayal. She didn't know what to think. Isola could not bring herself to tell the men who Marcel Palan was. Marcel Palan was her father, decades older than this imposter named Cruz. She didn't even know if this guy's name was really Cruz. She vaguely remembered the owner of the furniture factory, Bill Davis, had said something about Cruz's picture not matching his name. Perhaps he had been using her father's identity all this time and hiding it from her. There were so many things he'd lied about. She watched him casually walk away from the men surrounding her. Cruz wore the khakis and blue button-down shirt she had bought him. He had taken the time and cunning to steal and alter her father's papers. She realized she didn't know much about the man she had fallen so hard and fast for. In fast flashes more details about Cruz coursed through her mind: the key, her mother's ring, Josefina warning her about him, and her exchange with Bill Davis at the furniture factory—he had also warned her against Cruz.

Cruz looked hard at her. She could tell he wanted to know if she'd blow his cover. Instead, she wanted to blow *him* away, but she felt too paralyzed to do or say anything. Isola gave him her most virulent eye darts, a gaze that expressed all the anguish and loathing she had ever felt in her life. She strove to reflect back his total betrayal, but was interrupted by the police asking for her ID. Cruz reached her mother's house. He turned around and motioned for her to call him. He cradled an invisible phone in his ear. She remembered she had left her cell phone at the house. Isola wanted to throw up. He was the last person she'd call. Images of all the times that she had scoured the house for that ID card flooded her mind. How poor Josefina had pestered her for the mica! Stay present, she told herself. Don't faint. How many times had she lain in bed with Cruz, telling him about how hard she had looked for her father's papers. How many times had she turned over her mother's files, boxes, drawers—hoping to find her father's identification cards? Did he have her father's birth certificate too? Cruz's betrayal penetrated deeply; the taste of his deceit lingered in her mouth. She was too choked up to hear the men yelling at her. They wanted her identification. She was too upset, both at Cruz and at these policemen, to answer.

"Ma'am. Do you have identification?" The tall blur in a black T-shirt, brown hair, brown eyes spoke to her.

"I don't have ID," was all she managed. She wanted to dissolve, evaporate into the dry air. She stood there and allowed the heat to seep into her skin. The blood drained from her face. Her feet were firmly planted as she saw two more officers on bicycles circle and indicate that they were finished. Without further discussion, the officers shoved her in the back of a white van with half a dozen other people who seemed just as bewildered as she was. Isola allowed herself to be squeezed in with the others. Mexicans like her. Undocumented or perhaps citizens like herself. She had a hard time believing she was being mistaken for an undocumented person. She looked down at her clothes. Cruz's T-shirt, her mother's gardening Keds with holes exposing her mismatched socked toes. She looked ridiculous. She didn't have her wallet or cell phone, only her house key. Did that count for something?

She hoped she would be OK once she found her voice and was able to demand to speak to her lawyer. It hurt her that Cruz had been memorizing details about her while he was romancing her own mother. Her mother. She remembered him asking about her braces and tickling her teeth with his tongue. She had never experienced laughter so richly and didn't think to stop and ask Cruz how he knew about her braces. Her teeth were straight enough, and she hadn't worn her retainer, but it wasn't obvious. She knew she had never told him about her three years "with train tracks on her teeth"—that was something only her mother knew about. None of her adult friends or acquaintances from college knew. And then there was the fact that he had kept her father's identification card hidden from her. That was the worst. What exactly did he want from her and her mother? Was he trying to steal her inheritance too? Cruz's name hadn't come up in any of her mother's papers, so she knew her inheritance was safe. For now, he seemed simply to have womanized her family and stolen her father's identity. Her father was the most sacred person to her. She quivered with disgust all over again. A bump in the road caused the van to lurch forward, forcing the woman packed next to her to grab Isola's arm. Isola saw that the young woman was frightened. The woman stopped squeezing, but kept her hand on Isola's arm as if in a plea.

"I'm from México, but my son is not a wetback." She spoke the Spanish words as though sensing that Isola didn't belong there, either. "Él es nacido en Phoenix y mi hija también. Ella trabaja aquí y habla inglés." She talked frantically about her children, how they were citizens of this country, born and raised in Phoenix. Her daughter also. She works in town and speaks English.

"Shh, it's OK." Isola cooed and tried to quiet the woman down. "I can talk."

"¿Cómo?"

"Nothing. It's just that I was so scared earlier, I couldn't speak."

"I'm scared too," the woman said.

Isola put her fingers to her lips. She heard voices from the front of the van and wanted to hear what they were saying. The officers were arguing. They yelled something about "casting a wide net" and the "cost outweighing the benefits." The officers had screwed up big time and they knew it. But they didn't care that they were rounding up people like cattle.

"They're going to kill us." The woman started sobbing.

"No way! No es cierto. Soy Isola Palan." She extended her hand, tried to calm the woman down, tried to convince her she would be OK.

"Amalia Chávez."

"Mucho gusto. No te preocupes. Don't worry," Isola repeated.

Amalia started to pray, first an Our Father, followed by a round of Hail Marys. The others bowed their heads but said nothing.

Isola wondered why none of the four men talked to her. There was room in the airless van for two or three more people, but not enough ventilation for the six of them. The men didn't talk to each other. They all stared down at their shoes and seemed afraid to eye Isola and Amalia.

Isola didn't know what was going on, but she was certain Amalia was mistaken. They were being taken to jail and not to the border to be deposited in the middle of the desert with no water. Then again, none of the people in the van had handcuffs. And the last time she had checked, it wasn't a crime to walk around your neighborhood without a wallet.

Did Amalia know something Isola didn't? Amalia's small hands were smooth and dark. She was much younger than her worried face and tired voice suggested.

Isola reached into her pocket. She didn't have her phone. She remembered Cruz motioning to call him on her cell phone, the one she had left at home. She didn't have money or her ID, but she also hadn't done anything wrong or illegal.

Now Isola was able to speak to her lawyer, to the people that arrested her, but the van kept moving.

III

Ocotillo Dreams

30

History Repeats

Isola tripped as she rushed to use her one phone call from the Maricopa County Jail. She felt sorry for Amalia Chávez, who had no one to call, but she felt even lousier for herself. She tried to think good thoughts and calm herself as she flipped through the worn phone book for Liz Martínez's number while berating herself for being so stupid as to find herself on the other end of the bail line. Only days had passed since Cruz had called her from jail, asking her to pick him up. She thought about all the grief she could've saved herself if she had found out sooner that Cruz had stolen her father's identity. If she had sold the house to that couple Liz had found, none of this would have happened. No use worrying about that now. It's done. Isola promised herself that this time she'd sell the house and leave the desert ASAP. She prepared herself for another awkward moment as she explained to Liz Martínez why she needed bail. She thanked the clerk for allowing her to use the phone book and waited to be transferred to Liz's line.

"Liz. Thank God."

"I expected to hear from you days ago. Gabriela says your call is from the county jail. What happened?"

"Déjà vu," Isola whispered. Her conversation with Liz was way too similar to the one she had had with Cruz.

"Isola, what's that you're saying? Never mind, let me speak with the clerk and I'll come myself to bail you out. All I need to know is your unit and what the charges are. I'll get that from the clerk. You're obviously frazzled."

"Wait a minute! I also need you to bail out a friend, Amalia Chávez. She doesn't have papers or an ID."

"It's going to cost a pretty penny to bail her out."

"I don't care. I'll pay."

"Don't worry. My schedule's clear this afternoon. I'll be right over."

Although Isola was happy to get out of the detention center, she was even more touched to see that Liz Martínez had come to bail her out herself instead of sending her secretary. She motioned for Amalia to follow them to Liz's car. She seemed grateful for her generosity, but mistrustful of the lawyer. "Gracias, muy amable. Me voy en el bus," was all she said before exchanging phone numbers with Isola and the lawyer. Isola didn't blame her, but wished she had accepted the ride. According to Amalia, they were going in the same direction, only blocks away from each other. At least she had accepted Isola's offer to pay her bail. Isola hoped Amalia would follow through with a visit to Liz Martínez. Isola was willing to take care of her legal bills.

"You're just like your mother," Liz said.

"You obviously didn't know my mother well." Isola carefully opened the door of Liz's brand new gold Lexus.

"It's OK if you want to deny it." Liz's used her soft, placating voice. "I didn't mean to tease you after all you've gone through."

But Isola's anger rang out. "What's with this city and the police arresting people for not committing a crime? I wasn't doing anything but standing in my neighborhood."

"We've figured out exactly what's going on. It's called 'Operation Restoration,' something the City of Chandler and Sheriff Joe Arpaio thought up."

"Are you serious?"

"This is the fifth day of a wide sweep of arrests in order to catch illegals. The city of Chandler thought they needed to do their part to reduce the millions of illegals. They've picked up anyone with brown skin."

"It's 1997," Isola screeched. "Didn't we learn anything from the Japanese internment camps? They can't do that!"

"Technically, you're right, but they've done it. You aren't the only US citizen caught on this sweep."

"Wait. I remember hearing the cops talking about it. Their loud voices from the front of the van were muffled, but I heard them say something about casting a wide net, and that it didn't matter if they made mistakes."

Liz sighed. "It's nothing new. You haven't been around as long as I have. Eisenhower made up something called 'Operation Wetback' to remove 1.3 million illegals in less than a year, as if the word 'operation' made it OK to violate people's constitutional rights with blatant racial profiling. This time the city's been at it for five days and they're starting to feel a backlash from the public because they've made mistakes by detaining citizens like you."

"It better be a huge backlash," Isola said, still angry.

"Trust me. There will be." Liz turned to look her in the eye. A car honked and Liz gave the car her finger. "When we get to the office, I need to hear exactly what happened."

"What about Amalia?"

"With sponsorship and enough financial support, she should be fine. They let her go; that's a good sign. I'll need your full support to take on the city police. We also have important activists on our side like Juanita Encinas; she also knew your mother." They were stopped at a light. Liz turned to Isola. "You didn't purposely try to get caught. Did you? That's something your mother would do."

Isola turned to Liz and rolled her eyes, although secretly, she was proud of herself; she knew her mother would be too. She had been able to comfort Amalia and let her know that there wasn't anything to be afraid of. Those officers would've intimidated Amalia and denied her rights if she hadn't been there. Isola knew she was glorifying her small role in Amalia's troubles. She came back to reality upon their approach to Liz's office in the colorful border town of Guadalupe. The office was on the Phoenix side of the Yaqui Indian territory. The narrow streets shadowed by a vast mountain reminded Isola of the trip she had taken to visit her aunt Bernarda in México. Children milled around in the hot desert eating paletas and sliced mangoes on sticks with chili powder sprinkled on top. Most of the houses were neglected, with broken windows and torn screen doors, but the neighborhood had charm, with its colorful adobe bus stops and brightly decorated churches and shops.

"I can't believe the way the cops were talking about me as if I didn't speak English. Isn't it obvious I speak English?"

"No, it's not, especially in that outfit." Liz laughed. "Seriously, according to the charges, you did nothing to help yourself. You didn't even give the arresting officer your name the first time he asked. What did you expect?"

"I feel ridiculous in these cutoffs, but they can't arrest me for having a bad outfit and old shoes. Anyway, I'm not explaining myself. I'm still frustrated."

"As you should be. By the way, your mother was never a slave to fashion, either."

Isola started thinking of all the times she had been caught by a friend in sweats at the supermarket. She didn't really care what kind of clothes she wore. Here she was, literally walking in her mother's shoes, arrested in her mother's Keds.

"You're kind of quiet over there," Liz said.

"I was thinking about how helpless I felt when I was arrested. I knew they were talking about me, but because I was so mad at Cruz, I just stood there like a dummy." Isola stopped whittling a thread out of the bottom of Cruz's shirt. She had to face this awkward moment head on.

"Cruz. What Cruz? Tell me you didn't say Cruz." Liz did her arched eyebrow thing again.

"I did, but I don't want to get into it." Isola turned to look out the window.

"I hope it's not the Cruz I think it is." Liz's voice sounded sharp enough to break a crystal goblet.

"Dark, retro side burns, smile that . . ."

"That's Cruz." Liz spared her the awkward moment by screeching her car to a halt and turning off the engine. Isola followed Liz to her office. Liz stretched out her arms toward the sky and took a few deep breaths before turning to Isola. "You never mentioned him before."

"He was being so helpful and I let him stay at the house and . . ."

"You fell in love with him." Isola saw that Liz had figured everything out. She seemed sad and disappointed. Isola imagined her mother's face looking back at her and quickly pushed away the thought.

"You know about Cruz and . . ."

"Yes." Isola held up her hand to prevent Liz from blurting out the disgusting facts about her mother's affair with Cruz.

"OK, we won't go there. Was Cruz with you during the raid?"

Isola nodded.

"Then why wasn't he with you in the van? Did he outrun them?"

"Cruz stole my father's identity. When he identified himself as Marcel Palan I went numb. I lost my voice. That's why *I* was taken. Cruz walked away from the scene." Sudden tears streaked Isola's cheeks.

"You were in shock." Liz placed a box of tissues in front of her.

Isola grabbed a handful. "He probably has Papi's social security and birth certificate too. Cruz knew I had been looking for my father's documents."

Liz stepped out of her office and returned with two cups of water. She handed one to Isola.

"I need to tell you something, although you may not want to hear it."

"What?" Isola put the paper cup down and braced herself to have the discussion she knew she didn't want to have.

"Your mother wasn't proud of her affair with Cruz. She wanted to keep it from you. Cruz was supposed to stay out of your way. She believed the less you knew about her dealings, the better. But I think that talking to you about her affairs might've saved you from making the same mistakes."

Isola realized it was her turn to start talking, but she didn't know where to start.

"Are you going to press charges?" Liz looked straight at her.

"No." Isola turned away.

"Why not? Don't you want to be rid of him?"

"I don't want anymore dealings with the local police." She wanted a clean escape from Cruz. She didn't want to attract any more attention from authorities.

"I can understand you not wanting to press charges, but you need to make sure he leaves you alone. Do you think he'll keep pursuing you?"

"No. He won't," Isola said.

"Why didn't you tell me about him?"

Isola shrank from Liz's loud voice. "I . . ." Isola stammered.

Liz held up her flat palm. "You don't have to explain, but you've got to get those documents back. Are we agreed on that?"

Isola looked up at Liz. Her eyes were dry, but her voice sounded a little strained. "Is that buyer still interested in my mother's house?"

"I don't know. You've delayed so long. They might have found something else by now. But there will be others." Liz put a hand on Isola's shoulder.

"I noticed another house in the neighborhood sold in a day." Isola gladly changed the subject.

"It's a seller's market. But, Isola, you have to start trusting me and telling me everything. And you can't keep delaying the sale."

Isola nodded. She now had a better sense of how close Liz Martínez had been to her mother. "I will. Don't worry. And I'll get my father's documents back from Cruz." Isola spoke more to herself than to Liz.

31

Cactus Gift

Isola prepared iced tea for Josefina's visit. She recalled how rude she had been the last two times her mother's friend had dropped by. I owe her a big apology, she thought. Josefina had been telling the truth about how close she had been to her mother. And about Cruz. When Josefina had knocked on the door, Isola was grateful. She was not accompanied by her teenage nephew.

"You look nice." Josefina wasn't wearing the hotel uniform with her name on it, but sported a bright purple dress that showed off her shapely legs. She carried a cactus with small pink flowers forming a halo around the top of the plant.

"Gracias. It's my day off and we are having a fiesta for my mother's birthday. You can come. Mamá knew doña Marina."

"No, thank you. Would you like some iced tea or a cold soda?"

"Muy amable, pero me voy a la fiesta de mi mamá. Va a cumplir setenta y cinco."

"Seventy-five years old! How nice. Is that for your mother?" Isola pointed at the cactus.

"Este cacto se llama Isola. Your mother gave it to me before she got sick." Josefina handed her the cactus plant named "Isola."

"If it was a gift, keep it, please." Isola took a step back.

"No, I want you to have it." Josefina held the stubby plant up.

She gingerly took the cactus, holding it as though it would shatter at her touch. Isola didn't really want the plant. Her mother's game of naming plants after her daughter had been a rough spot between the two of them. Isola remembered playing in her room with her friends when her mother started carrying on long conversations with plants and flowers, all named Isola. One of her little friends snitched at school, and soon everyone knew that Mrs. Palan talked to plants and walls and lamps named Isola. The rumors died down only after Isola stopped inviting friends to come to her house to play. She retreated to the solitude of her bedroom while her mother talked to herself and the flowers. It took Isola years to renew her appreciation for plants, flowers, and gardening. "Mom always named her plants after me," she said, remembering that Josefina was also in the room. "Thank you." She took the cactus, placed it on the mantel, and handed the letter to Josefina. "I found it late last night behind the dresser." Isola shook her head. "I had been looking in the wrong place."

Josefina pulled out her glasses from her handbag and slowly read the brief letter as though savoring every word. Isola watched as Josefina lingered on her mother's words and phrases. The two sat in the same configuration as they had when they first met. She was on the long sofa and Josefina on the love seat, only this time she was not crowded by Josefina's nephew. Isola wanted to kick herself for not listening to Josefina in the first place. She had seen her as the enemy, wanting to leach off her family and sabotage her plans for Cruz. How narrow-minded of me, Isola thought.

"Está escrita en la mano de doña Marina," she said.

"Yes, the letter explains that my mother meant for you to have the mica," Isola stumbled on the words. "But Cruz . . ." She took a breath. "Cruz stole all of my father's documents. You've been so kind to me. I'm sorry I didn't believe you and that I was rude to you. I'm really sorry about everything." Isola grabbed a wad of tissue and blew a mournful trumpet that cut into choking sobs.

"Ay, niña. Cruz es un sinvergüenza. You were right. I should not have asked you for those papers. And Alfonso found a good job and they did not ask him any questions. Do not worry."

"Thank you. However, I do owe you an apology. You tried to warn me about Cruz and I didn't want to listen."

"I'm sorry you had to find out the hard way. Pero, la alemana didn't want nobody to tell you about him." Josefina stroked Isola's hair.

"You mean Gretchen? She knew about Cruz?" Isola turned to face her. "I guess that makes sense now that I can see more clearly. I found a picture of Gretchen and Marina walking in the desert, with Gretchen pointing at a cluster of purple wildflowers."

"La alemana era muy curiosa. When she came she covered her arms in long sleeves. The way she wore her clothes to avoid the sun made her look like la Llorona walking through the desert. I was embarrassed because I made fun of the way she dressed and I didn't know she could speak Spanish better than most of my relatives in México. She fooled us all. Doña Marina let her friend have the joke on us."

"Mom was fooled by Gretchen too. Gretchen used to teach Spanish. When did Gretchen talk to you about Cruz?"

"La alemana told me that your mother had complained about Cruz before her illness. Doña Marina worried you'd fall for him. We didn't think he would bother you. Hard to believe he had the nerve to show his face to you."

"Liz Martínez said something similar."

"I know her as well," Josefina said.

Isola realized Josefina wasn't the only one against her seeing Cruz. He had pursued her and it was impossible not to fall for him. She felt as though he had known her all his life. And in a way, he knew her intimately through her mother, and then through her own lack of restraint and common sense. Isola pictured her mother and Gretchen conspiring to keep him away from her. She remembered a comment Cruz had made early on, when they had first met. He said that she was the same as her mother. "Igual" was the word he had used. Isola had taken that meaning as an acknowledgement of how similar she looked to her mother, but evidently he was speaking of much more. Liz was right again. Her lack of trust and communication with her mother had been a tragedy.

"¿Señorita Isola?" Josefina stood up and waved her hand in front of Isola's eyes.

"I'm sorry. I'm daydreaming again and forgetting my manners. Can I offer you some iced tea, some cheese and crackers?"

"Disculpa, me voy a atender a mi madre."

"Yes, the fiesta. Have fun and thank you for stopping by. I want to make sure to see you again before I leave." Isola gave Josefina a warm embrace. She waved good-bye and immediately set about making plans for getting back at Cruz and reclaiming her father's documents.

She had had enough of his charm and puppy-dog eyes. Snapshots whirled before her. How she and Cruz had effortlessly made love in her mother's bed. How he had kept her father's ID in the leather wallet she had bought him because she felt sorry for Cruz's tatty and torn cloth wallet. How he had called her to ask for a rescue and bail-out for himself and Nacho and then had the nerve to leave with his friend. And how casually he had told her that he had gotten some other girl pregnant. Isola's entire being was repulsed by the thought that she had shared Cruz with her mother. She felt bathed in a sticky stew of repulsion. Her addiction to Cruz was as rational as a moth's attraction to fire. She convinced herself she was finished with him. "I'm over him" became her new mantra.

Isola continued to try to cut herself some slack. It wasn't the first time she and her mother had shared a man's love. But her father was a different story. Isola's relationship with her dad had been sweet, sacred, and nurturing. How dare Cruz steal her father's identity! Even her mother's inappropriate flirtations with Jeremy didn't compare to Cruz's violation. Her mother had liked to joke and tease her about how much she adored Jeremy, but it was in a maternal manner, and Isola knew her mother would never have slept with Jeremy. Cruz had pretended his relationship with her mother wasn't an important issue. She tried to breathe through the rippling ire coursing through her. She reminded herself she was at fault, too. Somehow, she should have suspected Cruz. After all, she had met him inside her mother's house and he had been at ease and comfortable with the running of the house. It didn't matter that he had at first refused the bed in favor of sleeping on the window seat. Of course he didn't want to be reminded of the bed he had shared with Marina. Enough, she said to herself. Think about how to get back at him.

32

Found Phone

Cruz was grateful for the pool and yard jobs in Scottsdale. It meant work for at least a week and a chance to step out of Pifi's pink-and-blue dollhouse. Epifanía no longer cared about curling her thick hair or buying nice clothes for herself. Every cent went to her baby. As he thought of all of his paychecks going to the baby, he again wondered if the child was his. He maintained his suspicion about someone else being the father. He wasn't sure why they needed to rope him into taking responsibility when there was that other man she was always with. He could see how her aunt could favor him over that güero tijuanero she sometimes ran with. Trinidad cared more about her niece being an unwed mother than Pifi did. Epifanía had never cared what people thought of her. The idea to follow her bachelor brother to Arizona was hers. Her family said it wasn't appropriate for a young woman to travel north alone. Her friends agreed that a female who left her town was scandalous, even if she was being escorted by her brother. Epifanía knew her friends were merely jealous of the opportunities she'd have.

Cruz opened his wallet, checked to make sure *his* mica was there. He didn't trust Trinidad or Pifi with it. The man from the restaurant had done a really good job of altering the mica, and the license had saved him from la migra. He was surprised Isola had covered for him and hadn't said a word to the policeman who had looked at both of them as if they were cucarachas crawling on his dinner. Cruz was also relieved Isola hadn't called him as he had asked her to. He took her cell with him, but had spent the rest of the day hiding at Trini's, afraid of getting caught. He was stupid to think he could do

159

anything for Isola. She'd be all right, he told himself. When la migra discovered that Isola wasn't a mojada, they'd let her go. They had to. ¡Qué jodida ironía! The irony of what had happened made him want to laugh. He held back his laughter, closed his eyes, and allowed a wide smile to spread across his face until something sharp tapped his back. The urgency of the poke, like a gun in his back, ruined the pleasure of his smile. He turned to find Epifanía holding Isola's cell phone and looking like the deranged homeless woman who hung out at la barda. In the past two weeks, Epifanía had made a habit of wiping away his smile.

"¿Pero qué te pasa?" Cruz remembered leaving the cell phone in his jacket pocket. He had been right about her searching through his things. "¿Por qué me esculcaste mi chamarra?" He pointed to his jacket and wondered what else she had found.

"And this?" Epifanía held the cell phone high in front of Cruz's face. Cruz thought she looked small, but fierce. "¿De quién es este celular? No es mío."

"Calma, princesa. Es de un chico en mi trabajo." Cruz studied her. He didn't think she knew much beyond the cell phone not being his, but she always seemed to know more than he gave her credit for. Her pout confirmed she knew nothing.

"Don't 'princesa' me and don't hide things from me. I heard all the messages and know this is 'Eee-zo-la's' phone. You called her for bail, instead of asking me or Trini for help."

"I'm not hiding things that are none of your business."

"I don't care if it's not my business. I still want to know."

"Ay, mujer. I thought I lost that phone." He kissed her forehead for being such a stubborn child, this nosy woman he was going to marry. "I'm going to work. Stay out of trouble and my things." He grabbed the cell phone from her hand and shoved it in his pocket.

She saluted him, turned on her heels and marched in an exaggerated stomp to her room. He was surprised and relieved she didn't put up more of a fight. He took a deep breath and left fast, allowing the screen door to slam hard behind him.

33

A Favor?

Epifanía didn't care that Cruz had left in anger. He had said the cell phone belonged to some guy he worked with, but she knew it belonged to a woman named Isola. At least her brother was respecting her wish to know the truth and had confirmed her suspicions about the Isola woman.

"Nacho!" She yelled. "Are you going to take me or what!"

"I'm getting the keys. What are you going to say to her? I'm pregnant, leave Cruz alone?" Nacho laughed.

"Shut up; just drive me to Isola's house." I'm going to say something like that, Pifi thought. "You should've told me where he disappeared to earlier. And about the bail money too, like I couldn't pay."

"Not that again. I don't get it about Cruz. Just cuz Vicente left you don't mean you need to take up with Cruz."

Nacho was on a roll, nonstop talking and criticizing. "I'm not listening to you." She put her hands over her ears. Epifanía kept her eyes on the road and studied the route Nacho took. She didn't want to look at Nacho's chata trompa and the way his lower lip disappeared underneath his big horse teeth when he was mad. Couldn't he do her one favor without complaining?

"You're going to listen." Nacho sped through a yellow light.

"Stay out of my business!" She turned and spat the words at his cheek.

"Cabrona, misses-stay-out-my-business. You want me to turn the car around?"

Epifanía's eyes flinched at the back of Nacho's hand raised high. She gripped the edges of her loose T-shirt. Nacho had never hit her. Not even when she had teased him about his big teeth. He had always forgiven her. Ever since she had told him about the baby, he had been more of a critic than a caring brother. She remembered how he used to save his pennies to buy candies and raspados; he even used to share his toys with her. Once he only had enough money for one lollipop. Her brother allowed her to pick the flavor, strawberry. The two used the clock in the kitchen and sucked on the candy for equal amounts of time, until finally Nacho let her eat the small red stub left after fifteen minutes of giggling and savoring the candy. She also remembered how nobody ever messed with her because the boy with the horse teeth would pummel them. Nacho punched with a fury. He didn't care about fighting bigger boys or having his teeth knocked out. He was her protector until she had started liking boys and stopped asking for his help.

"You fixed it so Cruz didn't marry Rosalina," he went on. "You're not going to rest 'til you get him to marry you and be father to your bastard."

"Shut up. He is the father. You're only talking shit because you bought this junky used car."

"Hey, I didn't have to drive you. We're here. Let's see what you're going to do." Nacho turned the car into the gravel driveway.

"You're not going to see anything. Wait here."

"You better hurry up. Don't waste my gas." He started the car back up, rolled the windows up and turned on the air conditioning.

"I ain't wasting no more of your nothing. I'll walk or take the bus home." She slammed the car door and walked quickly to the front door.

"Crazy huerca. Don't ask me to do you no more favors." He gunned the engine and peeled down the street.

Mamá had never approved of their fighting, but Pifi gave him the finger anyway. She didn't need Nacho. She saw that there was a bus stop at the corner by the shady park. She was good at taking the bus. They hadn't driven outside of Chandler and were only a few miles away from Trini's house. She convinced herself she was OK. No era nada. Trini would never know what she had been doing. It was Saturday. Trini would spend the rest of the afternoon visiting her comadre.

A woman with short black hair cut around the ears the way her mother used to trim her hair with a plastic bowl, opened the door. Pifi laughed, remembering how she hated those bowl haircuts. And here was this grown woman, probably a few years older than she was, wearing a little girl's hairdo. She didn't know what to say to this slim woman whose eyes were light like her own, but more speckled with green than brown.

"Isola?"

"Aah, you knew my mother. Come in. Too hot for formalities."

The woman named Isola grabbed her hand and pulled her into the living room before she could say she didn't know her mother or introduce herself. Isola motioned toward the couch. She returned with two glasses of lemonade.

"I don't want to sit down and I don't want anything from you." She stepped away from the tall glass Isola offered. "I just came to tell you I'm having Cruz's baby."

"Wait a minute. You're . . ."

"I'm Epifanía."

"Epi-pha-ny," Isola said slowly. She seemed lost in her thoughts as though she was trying to remember where they had met before.

Pifi thought she heard Isola saying Cruz's name or cursing him under her breath.

"Epifanía," she repeated. "Call me Pifi."

"Cruz's Pifi," Isola said softly.

The air-conditioned living room and Isola's quiet manner chilled her nerves. Epifanía had been prepared to fight for Cruz, but this woman welcomed her and didn't seem at all disturbed to see her at her house. "I should not bother you," she said.

"Don't worry. Sit down. Cruz told me about you."

"He did, when?"

"The day he called me to bail him out and then didn't want to accept a ride from me. Stupid, huh?" She pushed the glass of lemonade in front of Pifi.

"He could've called my tía Trini or my cousin or me." Pifi gulped half the glass of lemonade. She lifted the glass in a small salute to Isola. Pifi was surprised, but happy they were in agreement. She was embarrassed by the attitude she had walked in with. "Why did you think I knew your mother?"

"My mother died and her friends have been coming here. You're nodding. You know how that goes?"

"When someone dies, people have to come with their flowers, their food, their stories. They want to tell you how sorry they are, like you really need to hear all that from people you barely even know."

"Tell me about it." Isola said. She poured more lemonade, raised her glass and touched it to Pifi's.

The clink of the glasses reminded Pifi of how much her mother loved her tequila. "My mother recently died too. I wanted to see her before." She had trouble finishing her words. She had come here to claim Cruz for herself, not accept pity from this woman. Pifi used the napkin on the coffee table to dry her eyes.

"I'm sorry," Isola said.

Epifanía noticed how her pregnancy was affecting more than her growing belly. She remembered a time when she would've fought a woman to lay stake on her man. When she was a little girl, she used to fight for any reason, for toys, for candy, for her scrawny friend Magda, who was always getting picked on. Poor Magda who was run over by a car that didn't even stop to take her to the hospital. She said a silent prayer for her childhood friend. Epifanía no longer wanted to fight for a man like Cruz, especially with a woman with such sad eyes. Isola reminded her of her cousin Vicky in Atlixco. How she missed Vicky and wished she could see Vicky's two little girls, Analia and Xiomara. Pifi almost wanted to tell her that she wasn't exactly sure the baby was Cruz's, but she didn't say anything. Epifanía looked around the empty walls of the big house. Isola had a faraway look on her face. She touched her thumb to her index finger, closed her eyes and exhaled slowly.

"Do you do yoga?" Pifi asked.

"You recognized the breathing?"

"Sí."

"Do you practice somewhere around here?"

"One time, Adele, my boss, took me to a class at her gym. I enjoyed it, but I can no longer go. I'm too busy working." Epifanía rubbed her belly.

"How long have you worked for Adele?"

"Since I came here. I was fourteen when I started cleaning houses. It's a good job and Adele treats me like family."

"Are you going to school or college?"

"No, I don't need any special training to clean houses. Adele says I'll always have a job working for her. Maybe someday I'll have my own cleaning agency." Epifanía no longer had anything to say to Isola. She saw that Isola was packing everything in big boxes. "Are you selling the house?"

"Yes. Are you and Cruz looking for a place together?"

"My tía Trini is giving us a room until Cruz finds a better place."

"I'm sure you'll be happy together," Isola said.

"I've known Cruz all my life. He's like . . . Never mind."

"It's OK," Isola said. "You don't have to explain anything to me."

Epifanía listened to Isola's words. She felt foolish all over again for thinking Cruz was such a special prize. "How long did your mother live here?" Epifanía wanted to think of something other than Cruz.

"Marina moved here after my father died. And . . ."

"Your mother was doña Marina? I've heard her name, but . . ." Epifanía stood and gave the sweaty glass to Isola. Her lips mouthed a shy "thank you." She didn't like what she was hearing, or what she was thinking. "Can I use your telephone to call my brother for a ride?"

"I can take you home. I don't mind." Isola took the glasses to the kitchen.

"No, gracías. It's not far. I can walk or take the bus, but my head hurts. And I want to call Nacho."

"It sounds like you and your brother are very close."

"Yes, I tell Nacho everything."

"Please, let me take you home since you say it's not far."

"Thank you." Epifanía worried that Nacho was no longer at Trini's. She was grateful for not having to walk.

Isola's rental had a new-car smell. It was nice riding in a clean car. Nacho's car smelled like the musky cologne he used. Epifanía looked past the ripples of heat at Chandler Boulevard, a perfectly paved street so different from the roads in Atlixco. The clean and empty roads made her realize that Cruz was a man no one but she wanted. Rosalina obviously was happy with Diego and had long forgotten about Cruz. Isola may have had something with him, but she was leaving and didn't seem bothered by losing him.

"Do you know if you're having a boy or girl?" Isola asked as they drove.

"It's a girl. My tía saw that my belly was low and wide, not pointed high for a boy. When Adele took me to the doctor, they did the ultrasound and I saw my daughter for the first time."

"You seem excited."

"Yes, I really wanted a girl. My tía was hoping for a boy because she says boys are easier than girls. Turn here." Epifanía spoke quickly, in time for Isola to turn onto her street.

"Girls are more fun," Isola said. "You do live close by."

"Thank you for the ride." Epifanía waved to Isola as she drove away.

Epifanía sat on her aunt's porch and thought about how Trini hadn't asked any questions when Epifanía had told her the baby was Cruz's. She didn't really know what fulano got her pregnant. It either was the nice viejo she cleaned for in Scottsdale or Vicente, who disappeared forever, or that one time with Cruz. Híjole. The things she had to do for the sake of appearances. But what did it matter now that her mother was dead? Epifanía felt guilty for thinking such thoughts and for feeling free of her mother's watching eye. It was the same feeling she had had when she had first crossed the desert. Mamá was in her own world in México, and she was free to do whatever she wanted. At least until the phone calls started coming and she felt she had to account for almost everything she did. However, deep down she knew that she'd never completely sever the tie to her mother. As an angel in her glory, her mother watched down from heaven and saw everything.

34

Turning a Corner

Isola drove down Chandler Boulevard. The street was devoid of pedestrians, a ghost town of air-conditioned cars and buildings. Snippets of conversation rang in her head. Josefina's timid voice. Epifanía's youthful expressions. Words she had exchanged with Cruz when she had first met him. She wanted to drive to Papago Park to process all of the information she had received in the past six weeks. Visits from Josefina and Liz Martínez told her to act quickly and finish up her dealings with Cruz. She continued to replay all the verbal and silent messages from all the women who had told her not to give in to him. In replaying each scenario, one thing was certain—she had to teach Cruz that he could not use her the way he had used her mother. Or use women period. Isola knew that if Cruz had his way, he'd maintain his affair with her while playing house with Pifi.

Isola felt sorry for young girls like Epifanía who had to exchange their youth for the drudgery of cleaning other people's houses. Epifanía's posture and her tough claim on her man reminded Isola of the kids she had taught at the city college. College girls who had wanted to play grownup. Only Pifi had never gone to college and probably hadn't gone to high school, either. Her boss Adele had plucked Epifanía at the right age to convince her she could spend the rest of her life cleaning houses. Poor girl.

The afternoon traffic weighed down Isola's thoughts. For being in the desert, she sure spent a lot of time in her car. She didn't lose any time in planning her revenge on Cruz. If Cruz approached her for one last sack session before assuming his so-called responsibility, she'd teach him something about responsibility. She thought about giving Cruz a taste of his own medicine, while making sure she took back what belonged to her. You have to be more cold-hearted than you've ever been in your life, she told herself. You can do this. Cruz always slept so soundly after their lovemaking. His satisfied mouth opened wide and his snores trumpeted throughout the hollow house. She could do anything to him, tickle him, jab his sides; he'd still sleep in disgusting comfort. The bumper sticker in front of her read COUNT YOUR BLESSINGS. She counted her blessing of solitude in the sea of noise and motors. You can do it, she repeated to herself.

Back at the house, she ran up the stairs and was relieved to see that everything was as she had left it. Cruz had pulled off his last stunt. Liz Martínez's metal-sounding voice boomed in her ears. Her long-winded explanations about how much trouble she'd be in for simply not warning authorities that those documents were missing and that she knew that he possessed them made her feel like an idiot. She wanted to kick herself hard. Calm down. It's OK. She reminded herself to breathe. She turned on the radio in the upstairs bathroom and left it tuned to the oldies station that her mother and Cruz had enjoyed. Cruz didn't speak much English, but he hummed along and knew the tunes to many songs from the '50s and '60s. She took the pewter knight she had brought from her apartment in San Francisco and rubbed it for good luck. My knight will protect me, she thought.

She took the key from her wallet and opened the tin safety box with her mother's documents. Again, everything was in place, even the joint, triple-wrapped in plastic with a card that read "for emergencies only" in a scratchy handwriting Isola recognized as Gretchen's. And this was an emergency. She imagined Gretchen's gray, fluffy bob and soft grandmalike girth, but had a hard time picturing her and her mother sharing a joint.

Isola had seen the inside of an Arizona jail. She wasn't taking the chance of transporting the drug out of state for sentimental purposes. Isola remembered how angry she used to get with her parents for smoking pot in the attic. "You're not supposed to be doing that," she'd yell. "I can smell it." She had made her thirteen-year-old voice sound firm and authoritative, but only heard her mother's giggles through the walls.

She placed her mother's birth certificate and driver's license in a plastic bag and tucked it in the bathroom drawer. She had to trust that Cruz was still carrying her father's doctored papers in his wallet. Isola knew he thought his wallet the safest place for all his important papers and his money. He didn't trust banks. If Cruz dared to show up, she would be ready for him.

She flipped the photograph of her father to face away from her. She had found the picture two days ago and thought the cedar chest of drawers an appropriate altar. The turned-around frame looked as lonely as she felt. She heard the first three bars of the Rolling Stones' "As Tears Go By" and flushed the joint down the toilet. She closed the tin box and put away the stacks of folders. She remembered to add a twenty to the bag with the documents. In case Cruz discovered her checking his wallet, she'd use the excuse of giving him money. He had come to expect the extra bills. Cruz at first had seemed embarrassed by her giving him cash, but they had both gotten over the awkwardness of the situation.

Isola thought long and hard about her plan. She had everything in place except how to see Cruz one last time. She sat on the bed, leaned back, and tried to block out the radio voices. The oldies station was starting to annoy her because it had stopped playing music. Instead the DJ was taking insipid requests for birthday and anniversary wishes, sappy love declarations, and song dedications that made Isloa want to gag. "To my one true love, Ben. I'm yours forever, Becky from Queen Creek." Isola wasn't in the mood for all that mushy stuff, but the calls gave her an idea. Of course, call him, she thought. It was ridiculously simple: Cruz had her cell phone. All she had to do was call him and mention the phone. She had no doubt he'd return it, provided he hadn't lost it or the phone's battery hadn't died. She counted on Cruz's warped sense of doing the right thing, another notch on his belt of responsibility. Besides, her cell phone contained numbers and important information that were useless to him, and it wouldn't work unless she paid the bill. There was no reason for him to keep it. She went downstairs to the kitchen and dialed her number. Cruz answered on the first ring.

35

Save the Last Dance for Me

He had bought a single red rose from a man who wanted to sell him his last dozen, but thought twice about presenting it to Isola. She no longer seemed easy to please. The whole dozen might've made an impression. Instead, he had bartered for the one rose. Useless, he thought. Isola always said he smelled of flowers, and she especially liked roses. He cut the rose from its stem and rubbed the petals into his armpits and on his hair as he walked to the bus stop. He was so quick about it that someone walking by might think he was wiping the sweat off his body with a paper towel. The petals blew like black flies swarming away. He practiced his apology as he walked, inventing ways to tell Isola how sorry he was. He regretted leaving her to fend for herself with la migra. He didn't think the police would be so cold as to arrest the half-gringa-U.S. citizen and let the mojado go free. Qué ironía había en los Estados Unidos. Cruz almost wanted to laugh, but he wanted Isola to forgive him for taking her father's papers. He thought she was so close to understanding him that she'd give him the papers, and in a moment of weakness, he took matters into his own hands. Josefina kept meddling into his business and there was no telling what Isola would've done had Josefina had her way. Isola probably would have forgiven him for taking the mica if Epifanía hadn't pinned her baby on him. He wasn't sure what he was doing. No amount of regret or apologies would make Epifanía and the baby go away. He had ruined his chances at happiness with Isola, a happiness he didn't deserve. He was convinced there was only one way to right all his wrongs and that was to accept Epifanía and the baby.

Cruz started apologizing before Isola fully opened the door, but she didn't seem willing to listen to him. She stared blankly past him to the street. "¿Qué quieres?" she said. She left the door open and went into the kitchen. He stepped cautiously inside and followed her. He reached into his pocket for her cell phone and put it on the table, but Isola didn't seem to care about it. She poured rum into a tall glass. He was surprised she had been drinking. "Take this." She held the tall glass with the tips of her fingers, with her arm stretched out as though she were offering him poison. He wasn't used to her being so strange and distant, but was grateful she hadn't turned him away. He took a sip. The drink was good, strong. He thought a woman in this state of mind either wanted to fight or make passionate love. His penis obeyed and he was ready. He took another long sip. At least she wasn't too upset with him. She wanted love and he wasn't dreaming. Her cold, blank stare turned into the warm smile he remembered. He pinched himself to make sure he wasn't dreaming and allowed the cold ice to tickle his teeth. He wasn't mistaken, and she hadn't started yelling or reprimanding him for all the ways he had hurt her. She's really different, he thought.

Isola refilled Cruz's drink three times. He wanted to tell her how sorry he was about everything, but the alcohol made him feel dizzy. He couldn't believe she wasn't angry at him. She motioned for him to follow her upstairs. She was quiet and seemed older and more serious, like her mother. She had never before reminded him so much of Marina's strong personality. She wore Marina's dress, the one he liked with the yellow flowers. She pointed to the bed. Cruz sat on the bed and watched her. She changed the music from oldies to even older music of Cuco Sánchez. She had more rum and cold glasses in the bedroom's small refrigerator.

"You're quiet. Are you mad at me?" Cruz sat back against the headboard.

"Yes, I'm mad at you. That's why I'm taking off my clothes." She threw the dress on the floor and slipped under the covers.

"I . . ." Cruz started to explain.

"Shh. I don't want to hear anything from you." She pointed to the bathroom.

He scooted off the bed. In the bathroom, he undressed, used the toilet, and rinsed himself off in the faucet. He gargled with mouthwash and opened the door slowly. He was surprised that she was waiting for him. Cruz slid under the covers next to her smooth body. They made love. He came quickly. She got up and told him she'd be back in a second. She took her time in the bathroom.

"Did you get lost? What are you doing?" He tried to sound playful and hurt.

"You'll see." She yelled from the bathroom. He heard water. *Was she showering?*

Isola reemerged with a dark red lipstick, a color he recognized.

"I like that color."

She grabbed a black robe from the dresser and put it on before getting in bed.

Her gaze was so hard, Cruz thought she was putting an evil spell on him.

"I knew you were mad at me. I was worried," Cruz said.

"Worried?"

"Yes, worried."

"You should be worried. This is the last time I'm letting you in the door." She continued to stare him down.

"But we made love. You can't be too mad." Cruz tried to smile.

"It wasn't love. You know it was goodbye."

"I can't believe this. What kind of woman says goodbye like this? You're a crazy woman."

"I might be crazy, but you're more fucked up. You're here in my bed, but have you thought about what you're going to do about Epifanía and the baby?"

Cruz turned away from her. "You don't understand how it is."

"That's for sure."

"Part of me wants to go back to México."

"Great! That's not surprising, mister-I-need-to-take-responsibility. Abandoning your child is a great way to take responsibility. I bet you have a wife and kids in México."

"No, I don't. What's happening? Are you sick?"

"I am mad," Isola said. "Get out of my bed. Don't think about coming back. Es la última vez. And you better believe me when I say it's the last time."

Cruz quickly dressed and left. His head was throbbing. He wondered what she had put in his drink. He sure was wrong about her intentions. He stumbled onto the first approaching bus; he didn't care where it was going. He only wanted to get away from the crazy woman.

36

Papers Please

Outside the mini-mart, a tall officer smiled at him. Cruz recognized the smile. It said, "I'll arrest you no matter what." Ni modo.

"Marcel Palan." Cruz began to recite, but was nervous and wasn't sure the cop had even asked him a question. He said what he thought the cop had wanted to hear. The police officer asked him one last time. Cruz had long ago memorized Marcel Palan's social security number. He knew the uniformed man had it in for him, but he answered anyway in case he was just messing with him, as Nacho liked to say. The policeman used his index finger to motion for him to turn around. Cruz knew this was the part where he would frisk him and look at the things in his pockets and wallet. The officer used his radio and soon another Chandler police car with two more officers arrived. After checking inside his wallet, the officer handcuffed Cruz. He showed the mica to the other officers and they all laughed.

"The holding room's full." The stocky officer from the second car said.

"We can put him on the bus, cut through the paperwork." The three officers argued about what to do with him.

Cruz didn't understand what was going on. They laughed some more before shoving him in the second car. The seats were hot and they left the doors open. He hadn't checked the contents of his wallet since before he went to Isola's. He didn't know if the cops had taken everything. The cops continued to laugh.

"He doesn't know," the skinny officer said.

"You think?" The cop who had arrested him at the bus stop also started laughing again, louder this time. They sounded like wild turkeys.

The tall officer tapped the other cop's arm. "I don't speak Spanish, but I know the difference between Marcel Palan and Marina Jiménez. The picture doesn't do you justice, either." They laughed again.

When Cruz woke up in the middle of the desert, the officers' words and laughter rang in his ears. He thought of home and hoped he was heading toward Atlixco.

37

Rescate Ángeles

The house was sold and Isola was finished with her mother's desert affairs. She set aside the boxes of clothes and mementos she'd take back to San Francisco. She was zipping up her last suitcase when the doorbell rang.

"You came to say good-bye," Isola said, although she knew Josefina had no way of knowing she was leaving. She gave Josefina a hug and welcomed her inside.

"You are going back to San Francisco?" Josefina inspected the row of boxes, bags, and suitcases stacked by the front door.

"My work is done here," Isola said. "I'm so glad you came. I wanted to find you before I left."

Josefina nodded. She seemed to understand what Isola was saying, but she had a strange look on her face, as though she wanted to stop Isola from leaving.

"Sit down. What's wrong? If it's about my father's papers . . ."

Josefina shook her head and waved away Isola's concern. "I didn't come for that. I came to tell you about the Rescate Ángeles."

"Rescate Ángeles?" Isola remembered Cruz had mentioned the group a few weeks ago. "I had wanted to ask you about them. Aren't they disbanded?" Isola poured water into two plastic cups and handed one to Josefina.

"Yes. We used to work hard to help people cross with safety." Josefina took a sip of the water. "Your mother was la mera ángel de Rescate Ángeles, the leader."

Isola drank in Josefina's words. She saw how Josefina's light brown eyes glowed red in the sunlight. Isola thought that Josefina's fiery eyes were more youthful than her wrinkled skin suggested. "Does Liz Martínez know about this organization too?"

"The lawyer helped a few times. She's not a regular member. She's too busy."

"I know how busy she is." Isola put her cup on the counter. "I wish you had said more about this the first time we met."

"Doña Marina told us not to tell you. She said you were busy becoming a professor, and had no interest, but I think I told you anyway."

"I guess you did, but maybe I didn't understand." Isola tried to solve the last pieces of the puzzle. She wondered why her mother was so impossible to figure out. "She told you about my studies?" Isola's voice cracked.

"Yes, she was very proud of you. Her daughter was going to be una profesora, she'd say. Did you finish your research on that French queen?"

"No, I need to finish a fellowship." Isola didn't have time to explain to Josefina about her fellowship and the ranks and hoops of academia. She grappled with Josefina's words and wondered why she was the last to know her mother had been proud of her. She had always thought her mother hated her academic work.

Hearing such intimate details about her own life from Josefina and Cruz made her feel as though she were losing her mother all over again. Isola had always felt betrayed by her mother's commitments to her family in México and her political causes. It never had occurred to her that her mother showed her love by allowing her daughter a wide berth of independence, which often felt like indifference. Her mother had given her choices. She was allowed to accompany her mother to meetings or stay home alone with Mrs. Sánchez next door. Isola had been given responsibilities, but at the same time had seen them as unfair burdens. Isola's head felt as though it was about to burst. She sat down and massaged her temples.

"I'm always upsetting you. I'm sorry." Josefina stood up and patted Isola's shoulders.

"No, it's not you. It's just . . ." Isola's voice sounded strange to herself.

Josefina found napkins by the plastic cups on the counter and brought them to Isola. She looked in the freezer and put some ice cubes in one of the napkins and motioned for Isola to use the pack on her forehead.

"Thank you," Isola said. She wiped her tears and blew her nose. The ice pack felt good against her hot forehead.

"Rescate has not been active since your mother's last trip." Josefina spoke slowly.

"Are you asking for a donation for Rescate? I can give you some money." Isola worried about how her words sounded.

"No. We are no longer an active group."

"When I didn't give you my father's mica, I told myself I'd help you should you ever need help with anything else. I can't join the group, but I can give you some money to continue Rescate Ángeles." Isola went over to the window seat. She saw that the rosebush Cruz had planted needed watering.

"I did not come here to ask you for anything, " Josefina stammered. "I came to give these to you too." She seemed to have trouble finishing her thoughts and explaining what she had wanted to say. "These are your aunt's letters to your mother."

"Bernarda." Isola took the stack of letters. She pictured Manuelita, Bernarda's youngest girl, barefoot and wearing Isola's favorite old clothes. How she used to hold a grudge every time her mother had suggested they send another box of her old clothes and toys to Bernarda and her kids. The pictures of Manuelita's dusty, skinny legs and the way Isola's clothes fit too loosely or too tightly on Manuelita hadn't done much to garner Isola's sympathy as a child. She never realized her mother had forced her to send the items because Bernarda didn't have money or a husband to help her with eight kids. Strange that her mother had never offered to explain the situation. Maybe she had tried, but had been so blind and selfish, her mother didn't waste her breath. She wished she could take it back and be the daughter her mother had wanted her to be.

Isola skimmed each letter. She recognized the stamps from México and the postal seal from previous letters from her aunt Bernarda. The contents surprised her the most. Her name was all over the correspondence between her mother and Bernarda. Marina had painted a saintly image of Isola. In the letters, Isola was the catalyst for wanting to bring her cousins to the United

States. She put the pile of her aunt's letters to her mother on the table and one from Marina remained sealed and unsent. She'd recognize her mother's flowery hand anywhere. She had come to the desert to find answers, closure, to understand her mother's choices. Now nothing made sense. Isola wondered why her mother and everyone else kept trying to protect her and keep her in a safe bubble. However, the safe bubble never failed to burst in her face. She opened her mother's unsent letter to México.

Isola read phrases in the letters that puzzled her: "We're working hard to get everything ready for your arrival," "Isola wishes you luck," "I know Isola will be a good influence on Manuelita," "Ramón can take care of himself," and "Isola is preparing a precious room for the kids; you can't imagine how hard she is working." Isola didn't know why her mother had never mentioned this plan to bring Manuelita and Ramón, or her involvement with Rescate. But it was like her mother to take it upon herself to decide what Isola should or shouldn't be involved in. She remembered finding the plane ticket to San Francisco in her mother's handbag. She suspected her mother's trip to Frisco had been meant as a means to explain her plans of having Ramón and Manuelita live in the San Francisco house. It was as though her mother had been preparing Isola for this moment all her life. A role she had been too selfish to accept. Isola handed the letter to Josefina, who read it as though she had already seen it.

"I helped Marina send a previous letter, almost the same as this one. You should send word to your tía and tell her Rescate has been disbanded, so she will not expect anyone." Josefina followed her to the window seat. "Your mother shared these letters with me so that we could help them, but the group is no more."

Isola continued to scan the letters. "I can't disappoint my aunt any more. You need to rally the Rescate members and tell them they need to make one more trip for Manuelita and Ramón. If they've seen the letters they'll understand."

Josefina shook her head. "Your mother was in charge. We don't have all of our members anymore. She was the one who paid the pollero y el coyote."

"I'll pay. Please! How much money?"

"Three thousand dollars. Fifteen hundred dollars each, paid directly to Zurdo, el coyote. Es mucho dinero, sí." Josefina seemed at a loss for words.

"Sí. You know who these people are. We can do work together."

"Are you sure? It's a lot of money. And you are leaving to San Francisco." Josefina said.

"If I pay, is there any way you can pick them up?"

"No. I can only make the arrangements with Zurdo and the pollero. You need to rent a van and pick them up. I can drive with you, but you will have to bring them back by yourself."

"I can do that. Thank you." Isola continued to skim the letters. "Thirteen!" She blurted the number as though it were a curse.

"¿Cómo?" Josefina said.

"Manuelita's just a kid," Isola said. "Isn't it dangerous for her to be crossing the desert? Isn't there an easier way?" Isola spoke and then immediately regretted her stupid questions.

Josefina stared hard at Isola. Her subtle Mona Lisa smile suggested she was too polite to laugh outright at Isola's naïveté. Josefina looked down at her watch and was silent for a few minutes. "Manuelita is thirteen," she said. "And, yes, it is dangerous for anyone to cross, but I was younger than Manuelita when I came with my father and everything went fine." She stopped and her face hardened. "You can call them and tell them to wait until Manuelita is older."

"Call them? No, I need to do this," Isola said. "Thank you for helping." She started to feel the weight of what she was asking of Josefina, and more important, of herself. Her cousins were going to need a home, a school, a mother. She spoke the words and accepted her calling. Her cousins deserved all the benefits she had had.

"Don't worry. Zurdo will be help with Rescate Ángeles again."

"How will I find them?" Isola had a dozen other questions for Josefina. "How will I find them?" was only the first. She felt her stomach start to knot again.

Isola now pictured herself lost and dehydrated in the desert, looking for her cousins and being abandoned by the coyote. Zurdo. His very name sounded shifty. This is crazy, she thought. I'm crazy. I had everything set to leave this forsaken place, this house of ghosts and ocotillo dreams.

"I'll drive to Naco with you. But you will be alone on the way back."

"Alone?"

"Yes. I won't be returning with you. Can you manage?"

She turned and saw in her golden eyes that Josefina was also determined to help Manuelita and Ramón. Isola felt ashamed of herself. People like her mother and Josefina sacrificed so much to help strangers. "Yes. I must help my family," Isola said. *Oh God, I'm sounding like my mother.*

"It is a good thing to do," Josefina said.

"Do we need anything besides the money for the coyote?"

"Extra water to leave in the Rescate drops, places in the desert where we leave bottled water for people who cross on their own."

"When do we need all this by?" Details about what to do with her luggage, her plane ticket, where to stay, how to get so much cash so quickly swirled in Isola's mind.

Josefina chose a letter from the bottom of the stack and read the translucent airmailed pages. She smiled the way Marina used to smile when she expected Isola to complain about an answer. "Mañana," Josefina said.

38

Ocotillo Dreams

Although Josefina had reassured her several times over, Isola didn't trust Zurdo. His face seemed as crooked as his name, which meant "Lefty." Isola wanted to study his eyes, but all she saw was the sweep of black hair and a scar that looked as though a hot iron had sealed a permanent crease on his cheek. She worried Zurdo might rob her of the extra cash she had stashed in her wallet. She reassured herself there were easier ways to rob her of the money. Forking over cash to a coyote was nothing short of highway robbery. So what difference did it make if Zurdo or some other creep took her money? Her cousins had the dangerous part, making the long, hard trek through the desert. The money didn't matter at all, she told herself. She had no choice but to put some faith in Zurdo. Besides, Josefina had told her he was a member of Rescate. She had already relinquished the driving to him, but followed every turn he made on the map and kept her eyes on the paper with the directions to Naco, the small border town she had never heard of.

The minivan jerked over rocks and potholes. The scenery was so similar that Isola had the feeling they had been driving in circles. She looked at the time, almost 4:00 p.m., and wondered if they'd ever reach Cochise County. They finally passed Tucson and reached the road to Naco. They stopped the van, but left the air conditioning running. Isola turned to check on Josefina, who had been asleep in the back since they left the Maricopa county line. Josefina opened her eyes, stretched her arms and legs, and flexed her feet.

"We wait here. Take out half of the waters and leave them here." Zurdo pointed to the nearest bush off the side of the road. Isola didn't want to get out because she didn't trust Zurdo and she didn't know what to do. She stayed in the van while Zurdo finished handing out the gallons of water to Josefina.

"How long do we wait?" Isola felt foolish for not helping with the water bottles.

"Until they come," Zurdo said. "If it's more than half an hour, I'm turning the air off."

"What's the most you've waited for someone?" Isola asked.

"Two days, for my wife. I don't wait that long for anybody else." Zurdo picked at his gold tooth with his pinky nail.

Isola didn't know if he was kidding or trying her patience. The first half-hour went by slowly. The air conditioning chilled Isola's legs. She didn't mind the cold. She wanted to remember the feeling of cool goose bumps on her thighs, of cold so chilly she felt feverish. Next came the sudden heat blast. Zurdo left the windows up until the air in the van turned stuffy, then uncomfortable. The sun was no longer so high and the desert glowed vermillion beyond the horizon. It's beautiful, Isola thought. She closed her eyes for a second, but was startled by Zurdo pulling binoculars out of a box.

"¡Josefina! Es hora." Zurdo tapped his wristwatch.

He tossed her a large pair of binoculars. Josefina came alive. She opened the van's door and put the lens to her eyes. Isola noticed how youthful Josefina looked in jeans and a black T-shirt and her long hair in a loose braid instead of her usual tight bun that made her face look as though her eyes were sliding off.

"I thought you said we were meeting them in a van." Isola said.

"¡Qué tipa tan estúpida nos trajiste!" Zurdo laughed at Isola.

Isola ignored his calling her stupid. She thought she deserved the insult for being so ignorant.

"Es la hija de doña Marina." Josefina silenced Zurdo's laughter. Isola watched them cross themselves at the mention of her mother's name. Isola joined their prayer by kissing her thumb.

Josefina tugged Isola out of the van. "We pick them up from the pollero. We are looking for people who may need help. Your mother wanted especially to assist women and children."

"You've been very patient with me, thank you."

Josefina put her arms around Isola's shoulders and gave her a squeeze.

"It's hard to understand our work here. We need to watch out for la migra y los Minutemen. Sometimes we yell into the bullhorn and tell people not to come out, to stay where they are if we see the vans or the jeeps of the Minutemen."

"I understand everyone is working against each other, rather than with each other. That's stupidity." Isola made sure Zurdo heard her.

Zurdo spat out the window.

Through the binoculars, Isola focused on a single fiery flower of the ocotillo. She remembered Cruz's dream.

It's a dream that is very ugly. I'm crossing la frontera. The sun is setting and it's a good time to walk. Farther in the distance I see a woman rocking back and forth, the way somebody tries to quiet a baby. Only the woman does not hold a child. She holds her arms close to her. As I walk toward her, I see she is seated beneath an ocotillo, a skinny cactus with several arms and red flowers at the tip of each branch. The red tips of the ocotillo are covered in blood that is dripping onto the woman's face. When I reach her, I have a strong feeling that I know her, but I don't recognize her because the blood is covering her face. Her eyes are open wide, como si estuviera asustada. She grabs my hand, whispers my name, and dies. Her scared eyes stare at me. When I see her eyes, I still don't recognize her, but I know I loved her. I always scream when she grabs my hand. Her fright becomes my fright. Her loss becomes my loss. I wish that dream would go away. Every time I wake up, I taste chocolate in my mouth. I think my tongue is bleeding, but it is not. This time I was not biting on my tongue.

Isola got a chill down her back thinking about Cruz's dream. The images of him biting his tongue and of the red flowers of the ocotillo were what had initially sealed her attraction to him. She knew Cruz would be forced to cross the desert now if la migra caught him because he no longer had her father's documents. Although he talked about going back home, she didn't believe he'd stay in México. Rescate had helped him cross the border. Isola knew Cruz would be on his own. She tried not to worry about him. He was cunning enough to alter her father's papers. He'd probably buy some other false documents with all of the money she had given him.

"Aquí están." Josefina clapped her hands together.

"Are you sure that's them?" Isola took a deep breath and tried to calm her nerves.

Manuelita and Ramón emerged from the white van that pulled up next to them. Manuelita reminded Isola of herself when she was younger.

184

Ramón was a darker, taller version of Manuelita. They both wore jeans and the same blue T-shirts. Manuelita had a sweater tied around her waist. They were sweaty and tired, but not as beat as Isola had expected. She had worried that she'd find them halfway dead or severely dehydrated. They were both so thin and fragile looking. Manuelita's pretty, Isola thought as she approached them. They stood looking at each other as if in disbelief that the other was real. Isola moved closer to them and the three embraced in an awkward hug that was more of a pat on the back.

Zurdo paid the pollero.

"Drink some water. There's sandwiches too." Isola opened the ice chest. "Eat." She encouraged them to take more than one sandwich.

"Gracias." Manuelita and Ramón were both hungry. They offered sandwiches to everyone else before tearing open the subs Isola had purchased. She was glad she had bought extras.

"I'm leaving with Zurdo after we eat," Josefina said. "I have important work with Zurdo and Rescate. Drive them straight to Liz Martínez's house. When you're ready, you can take them to San Francisco. I'll give you more instructions in three days." Josefina kept her eyes on Isola, as if imparting some of her own strength and courage.

"OK," was all Isola managed. She couldn't believe Josefina was abandoning her.

"Are we going to California, prima? I thought we were staying at my tía's house in Chandler, aquí en Arizona." Manuelita's eyes widened.

Isola nodded. Manuelita clapped her hands. Her enthusiasm was infectious. They all smiled with her. Isola loved seeing Manuelita so happy.

"Can Ramón bring his girlfriend?" Manuelita's squeaky voice cracked.

"You have a girlfriend?" Isola said. He was skinny and hardly taller or older looking than Manuelita. Isola had a hard time believing he was into girls.

"Yes, in Tucson. That's where I'm heading to," Ramón said in Spanish. "I was going to tell you, but this little big mouth beat me to it." He tousled his sister's thick hair and pretended to punch her arm.

"How is it you have a girlfriend over here?" Isola asked.

"She's from our town," Manuelita said. "She crossed with her family a year ago. She writes letters to us, too."

"What about you? Are you going to Tucson too? Do you have a boyfriend there?" Isola patted Manuelita's hand.

"No, prima. I'm staying with you. I've been dreaming about making this trip forever." Manuelita leaned into Isola's arm.

Forever is a long time. Isola remembered her mother's phrase. Her eyes started to water. She was sorry she hadn't helped her cousins earlier.

"La muchacha sí se parece a Marina," Zurdo said. He kept repeating how striking the resemblance was between Marina and Manuelita. Isola remembered her mother's words about her sister, "If Bernarda were skinnier, she would be prettier than me." The sisters looked a lot alike and, not surprisingly, Manuelita bore a strong resemblance to her favorite aunt. Isola knew it would be easy passing her off as her sister. She would have problems enrolling her in school and getting her caught up to her level. "I'll manage," she told herself.

Isola had so many questions for her cousins. She didn't know where to start. "Was it hard?" she said.

The two siblings were silent for a long while. They stayed quiet as though they were reliving the whole experience and telling about it telepathically.

She wanted a better word. "Hard" was an exam. "Hard" was trying to meet a deadline. Crossing the Mexican border and walking through the desert and leaving your mother and sisters behind was something more than hard.

Ramón began.

"I thought the desert would be hot, vast, and empty, only cactus and dirt," he said. "Pero no. There's people like la migra, y los Minutemen, small animals like rabbits and birds and prairie dogs. There's clothes, water bottles, and all the things people leave behind. Sometimes you see bones of animals. And I try not to think that I can be those bones left for others to see."

Isola gazed out into the desert. It looked tame from her vantage point and empty, as Ramón had anticipated.

"Manuelita, you must have been scared."

"She was good. She didn't cry or complain. I think we will have to call her 'Manuela' from now on."

"Nobody calls me that!" Manuelita complained.

Everyone, including Zurdo, laughed.

"The pollero wanted to scare us by showing us the dead man. He said it was the work of los Minutemen because they shot at the man's water bottle," Ramón said.

"We need to leave." Josefina put her arm around Manuelita.

"Huh? What man? The Minutemen killed him?" Isola covered her mouth.

"¿Quién sabe?" Ramón said. "There's no way of knowing for sure. He wasn't bleeding or wounded, but dead. It doesn't matter."

"It does matter," Isola said, "What did the man look like?" She leaned on the van. "Cruz," she whispered to Josefina before retching dry heaves. She continued to cough.

"Dáme el papel," Josefina said to Manuelita. She moistened folded paper towels and handed them to Isola. She ushered Isola to the other side of the van. "Drink some soda and put this on your forehead. Are you all right?"

"Yes." Isola pushed away the soda. Her eyes flooded with tears and she sank to the ground and cried into the wet paper towels.

"You need to get up," Josefina said.

"Is she all right?" Ramón asked. "I wouldn't have said anything about the man if it was going to upset her."

"He reminded me of the nice man who sometimes works at the corner store because of his long, thick hair." Manuelita piped up.

"¡Esta muchachita! She wasn't afraid to see a dead man." Ramón slapped Manuelita on the back.

"She takes after her tía," Josefina said. She gave Manuelita a big hug. She darted Isola a look that told her to compose herself.

"I need to know where you found him," Isola said.

"We found the dead man by an ocotillo." Manuelita seemed thrilled by the discovery.

"We need to help him," Isola said.

"He's dead, prima." Manuelita and Ramón spoke at the same time.

"Did he have a gold chain around his neck?" Isola grasped Manuelita by the shoulders. The girl started to cry.

"He had some gold, but I don't remember." Manuelita spoke between sobs. "Maybe a gold chain or a ring."

"I knew she'd start crying eventually," Ramón said. "There's hundreds of ocotillos in the desert and we weren't about to take gold off a dead man."

Josefina pointed her head toward Ramón and Manuelita. "Isola, we don't have time to look under every rock and cactus."

"But . . ." Isola felt paralyzed. She had only wanted to stop Cruz from taking advantage of her. Never in her scheme for revenge did she imagine he'd end up dead. In prison, arrested, maybe, but not murdered in the desert.

"You need to get them to Liz's," Josefina said.

"I know," Isola said. She felt lousy about her cowardly act. She could've just as easily gone to the police and let them deport Cruz, saving herself the possibility of endangering his life. She wanted to retrace the pollero's steps and look for the body, but Josefina was right. At this moment, she had to put her cousins first.

"Leave now!" Josefina put her hand on Isola's shoulder and shoved her toward the van.

Isola climbed into the driver's seat. Not knowing who the man was made her revenge on Cruz seem all the more cruel. Although the dead guy could've been anybody, she had a terrible gut feeling it was Cruz.

Josefina poked her head inside the van. "I'll call you if I hear anything about the man," she said. "They are tired. They need warm showers, more food and water. You wanted to do this, remember?"

Isola nodded. "Don't worry. I can do it."

They drove for hours and saw nothing but a blur of brown-and-green desert. Isola didn't recognize the towns they passed until they reached Tucson and Picacho Peak. When they arrived in Phoenix, Isola started to relax. She stopped at a McDonald's and studied the directions to Liz's house.

"¿Prima? On our way to San Francisco, can we stop at Disneyland?" Manuelita's voice squeaked as she said the name of the place that meant California and a better life.

Isola remembered her mother telling the story of how the first thing her young niece wanted to do in the United States was go to Disneyland. "Yes, sweetheart," Isola answered without hesitation. Her mother's voice echoed in her head.